MY NAME IS VITTORIA
Dafna Vitale Ben Bassat

To my father Aldo and my grate family

Vercelli
The Basola Family

I was pampered. This is what happens when you are raised with a mother that makes her own sausages; cooks the tomatoes until their scent is absorbed in the drapes around the house; and who picks her own basil, chops it up, and then adds a little to the sauce, strains it, and tastes.

"To prepare fresh pasta," she would say, "the kind that tingles on your tongue, you have to know," just like knowing by the softness of the tomato, if it is suitable for a bruschetta or a sauce."

These were the aromas I grew up with. The smell of piping hot coffee, the sharp scent of the shoe polish my mother would use to polish my dad's shoes, all mixed with the smell of freshly baked bread.

Alfredo, my father, always came first, and we came after him. He was the reason my mother, Anneta, got up in the morning. First her husband, and then her children.

I was born in Vercelli, a small town on the main road between Milan and Torino. It had a big fancy synagogue and a measly Jewish cemetery. I was born in the year Mussolini met his beloved Jewish girlfriend Margarita Tzarfati, the daughter of a Jewish aristocrat family from Venice. The streets of Vercelli, which were mostly paved with cobblestones, and the city square were the playground for my sisters, my little brother, Napoleon, and me. We would stroll in the streets and run around the *piazza* at dusk when the traffic of bicycles, carts, and the few cars we had in town slowed down. The *piazza* was a meeting place. Everyone gathered there in the evening; the men with a shot of grappa in the local bar, their wives chattering, keeping a watchful eye on the kids that were chasing pigeons. Only after sundown did the crowd disperse, leaving behind the scent of alcohol fumes lingering in the air.

I recall very little from my childhood, which is considered a good sign. I remember the streets and the smells. I was the second born after my sister, Celeste, and I remember my joy when my little sister, Bellina, was born and the great happiness when my brother, Napoleon, was born. My mother had quite a large pelvic, as she exercised very little. I remember she was always at home, reading or sewing, sifting through rice, or sorting green beans. She disliked the neighbor's chatter and loved waiting to welcome us when we came home. Very seldom did she go down to the store from which the smells of the whole world were carried up to us.

Our father's elder sister, Celeste ("pale-blue" in Italian), also lived with us in our spacious apartment. She knew Margarita when she was young and also attended her magnificent wedding that took place in Venice.

My father's store used to be a thrift shop, and once he married my mother, Anneta, he expanded his business and started selling mainly textiles. My mother showed no interest in commerce but was very interested in my father. On his part, he loved the traveling his business required and the meetings he had with women. The debate whether to sort the rolls of fabric according to color or brand became something of a habit for him and his big sister, Celeste. Every morning, Alfredo would roll up the heavy shutters, letting the sun in to light up the rolls of fabric placed in the window. At the back of the store, the cut-off leftovers and the damaged fabrics piled up, close to the dim stairs that led to our well-lit apartment.

My father, with his keen sense of business, was wise enough to purchase two apartments and join them together into one sparkling clean spacious flat, loaded with polished furniture. The kitchen faced the street and from its large window, my mother could see the comings and goings of everyone. My parents' bedroom was at the back of the house, and in between, were Aunt Celeste's room and the nursery, large and spacious with a huge closet. We girls would try on and change our outfits for hours, checking ourselves in front of the mirror, comparing waistlines and hip width. Three girls above a fabric store.

We were the proud owners of one of the most exclusive fabric stores in Vercelli. My father wasn't a socialist but wasn't anything else either. He was a handsome man with three daughters and a late-to-arrive son, an elder spinster sister, a successful store, and a healthy appetite for life. He adored the life of comfort, nice clothes, and pretty women. He was quite pleased with the sales of the green taffeta fabric, which shot up following the picture of the Jewish lover in her elegant dress taken at the celebrations for Mussolini's election to parliament.

In 1921, Mussolini was elected as a representative of the social party in parliament. He became known as the editor of the social party's magazine, and Margarita—his beautiful lover—was the ambitious art critic for that same magazine. The few Jews in Vercelli used to eagerly read the magazine brought to them by my aunt and to proudly gossip about the red-haired, green-eyed lover.

My aunt, older Celeste, had no husband or lovers. Although she was less pretty than Margarita, she knew more about art. She was a slender, handsome woman, with a stiff expression. Only when she painted on her white clay vases with light-blue, did a slight smile sneak onto her lips. On Mondays, Tuesdays, and Thursdays, she worked in our fabric store, and during the rest of the week, she taught at the Vercelli Art Center.

Older Celeste always had the final word on everything; even my father was a little intimidated by her. I believe that the essence of her entire existence was to be argumentative with a compulsory need to rattle my mother.

In actual fact, she was the one who ran the store, deciding what fabrics to bring in, counting the cash from the register at the end of the day, advising customers, and teaching us girls the art of selling. We all worked in the store—all but my mother, who was in the one place that mattered to her the most, the kitchen.

My mother wasn't much of a talker. She used to share her thoughts only with my older sister, little Celeste. They were allies, a tad aloof from Bellina and me. My name was chosen by Alfredo. He loved soccer and wished for a son, but had me. Vittoria, he called me, "Victory," and when my name is pronounced, a smile is left on one's face. My little sister, Lina—short for Bellina—was truly the prettiest, with blond hair, big eyes, and a permanent smile. My brother's name was Napoleon. That is how my father wanted it—Napoleon, the hero.

Right after Napoleon was born, a bathroom was installed in our apartment, and we stopped using the building's communal one. Having an indoor bathroom symbolized a social status that became my father. Every morning, he would spend time in there, making us all wait. It was only on the days he was away—or the nights he didn't spend at home for reasons I didn't want to dwell on—that we entered the bathroom according to age, Celeste first.

Celeste
(Light-Blue)

It was the week of my thirteenth birthday that mother and older Celeste closed me off in the kitchen and first explained to me about the little pieces of fabric that little Celeste, my older sister, would wash in hiding and hang on a separate clothesline.

"Your body is transforming from that of a girl to that of a woman. The womb is getting ready to receive the seed from which babies grow, and since you do not have the seeds yet, the body discards the preparation for it. The stomach pains you will feel are your body's disappointment. The more the blood flows and the pains of your cycle are more intense, the chance you'll be more fertile increases."

"Does it hurt when you bleed?" I asked my sister Celeste before she fell asleep that night.

"No," she replied. I heard her turning in her bed, but something in the way she answered prevented me from asking any more questions. I also wanted to ask if it hurt when the seed meets the prepared womb, but I couldn't bring myself to.

My big sister, Celeste, was kind but withdrawn. When she received a new dress or a new blouse, and Lina and I wanted to try it on, too, she would frown and say, "Not now, some other time," and would hide it in the back of her closet.

I remember the day I was invited to my best friend Alicia's birthday. I wanted to borrow my big sister Celeste's dress. She wasn't home, so I couldn't ask her permission. I opened the closet, saw the dress with the blue flowers hanging in there, still new and starched, calling out to me: "Let me out." Next to it, there were more of Celeste's dresses, kept for important occasions, and then I saw the gleaming white blouse with the lace collar. It was a new blouse she received from my aunt, which had never been worn. I tried it on; it looked nice on me.

As I said, Celeste wasn't home. Lina fixed my hair and complimented me, and my mother didn't notice when I kissed her good-bye. I went all spruced up to my classmate Alicia's birthday. Her entire family was there, cousins and a few girlfriends. We played rummy and ate cake, and when the time to go home was nearing, one of the uncles, who had quite a few drinks, got up staggering and laughing out loud, and headed toward the kitchen. I looked at him, smelling the alcohol fumes in the room, and wished to leave and go home. I tried to be polite. I took the plate with the stale leftover cake that had been served on it and went to place it in the kitchen.

I saw him there, trying hard to forcibly open another bottle of wine. I placed the plate in the sink, turned around, and a gush of wine splashed all over my face and body.

I bid my embarrassed friend farewell and walked the two blocks toward our house trying to assess the extent of the damage. The blouse was entirely stained by wine, the collar, too. My sister Celeste hated when someone borrowed her clothes. It would be impossible to go straight into the laundry room without passing through the living room, and it would be impossible to hide the theft and the ruining of her blouse. The blouse would never be white again, and she had never worn it. Any outburst of anger coming would be justified.

As I walked, with the scent of wine in my nostrils, I saw from the street that the house was darkened. There were days when everyone turned in early, and I hoped this was one of those days. The store's blinds were shut, and the time was quarter-to-nine in the evening. Not only was I half an hour late, but my sister's new blouse also had wine all over it, too.

I opened the door. Sitting in the living room were my Aunt Celeste; Alfredo, my father; my big sister Celeste; and Lina, my younger sister. My mother's voice could be heard from Napoleon's bedroom as she read a bedtime story to him.

Everyone looked at me, and Alfredo asked, "Where were you Vittoria? You started bartending? You smell like a brewery."

"I am so sorry Celeste," I said directly to my sister, who wasn't even looking at me.

She looked at me with an inquiring gaze, and when she saw the blouse, she lay down her sewing kit and turned red. She got up and slapped me across the face.

My aunt put down her paper. Lina, who was sitting on the sofa, hugged her legs. My dad got up to pour himself a drink and seemed quite amused.

Despite the red sensation on my cheek, I said what I planned to say, "I am so sorry. There was a birthday party; I wanted to ask you for permission, but you were not at home. There was this drunken uncle there who spilled wine all over my blouse, I will try and wash it immediately. I am really, really sorry."

I tried the truth and continued without breathing, "You were not at home so I couldn't check if you would allow me to wear your blouse. I initially wanted to take the dress, but then I saw this blouse that you've had for almost a year and haven't worn. I thought you didn't like it."

This was already too much, unplanned and unnecessary. It caused her to turn back from her place, stand up in front of me, and say, "You are a liar, and you'll always be a liar. You knew I wouldn't let you wear the dress or the blouse. I kept this blouse especially. From now on, if you even come near my closet, I am cutting your clothes. For every item you take, I will cut one of yours…"

Her eyes were blazing. She looked at my aunt, who nodded in affirmation, and at my dad, who was pouring himself yet another drink, to check if she had enough venom in her voice, and continued, "You saw that I wasn't home, so you stole my blouse. This is not the first time. If this idiot hadn't spilled wine all over it, you would have put it back in the closet without me knowing. You are an obnoxious sister and a user."

She was right. From time to time, because she was so stingy, I took clothes from her closet. Wasn't it a shame that they just hung there with no one to enjoy them…

Hearing our voices, my mother came into the living room with my brother Napoleon tagging along behind her, calling, "What happened? What happened?"

When she saw Celeste and me with the white blouse that was now stained, she said tiredly, "Put the blouse in the laundry room; we will try to save it. And you, try to be a little more generous, and no one will steal from you. Now both of you quiet, Napoleon needs to sleep."

"It is red wine and more than fifteen minutes have passed," my aunt said annoyingly quiet. "The blouse will never be white again. Maybe try salt and cold water before you wash it."

She collected the dishes and went to the kitchen as she gave me a frightening look. I knew she also thought I didn't always tell the truth and that she sided with Celeste. Something about having the same name connected my aunt and my big sister.

During the night, I hugged Lina and promised her she could borrow my clothes any time she wanted. She moved into my bed and tried to comfort me. Celeste's words echoed in my head. It's not that I was a liar; it's just that my imagination was much more developed than hers. It was important to me that reality not become so boring. If a customer walked into the store and did not purchase anything, as far as my sister was concerned, she "did not buy anything." I would make up a story: that her husband wasn't making enough money or perhaps she didn't think that purple suited her, or maybe she believed that blue would bring a disaster upon her.

I didn't like lying; I loved to be heard... I felt contempt for my big sister, who was so stingy with everything and didn't have the need to be heard or loved.

In the textile store, there was a pair of cutting scissors that were tied to the big table by a rope. Only after measuring with the large wooden ruler and marking the fabric with white chalk was the fabric ceremoniously cut. When we were kids, we were not allowed to cut. I would wait for older Celeste to finish with the customer. Then she would approach the big wooden table and examine whether I measured correctly so no fabric would be wasted.

That morning, I was the only one in the store. My sister, younger Celeste, was in the kitchen watching over the meatballs and the *fagiolini* that had been cooking since morning. Mother went with Napoleon to buy spices, as we were out of basil; my father went to buy merchandise out of town; and older Celeste was teaching in the academy as she did every Tuesday.

On that cold Tuesday morning at the beginning of January, *Señora* Ivona Augusto came rushing into the store. She needed a few extra meters of the green fabric she had bought a few days ago—a special, wild silk that my dad, Alfredo, brought in only about a week ago. I hoped that some would be left from that fabric so Mother could sew a blouse for me. The refined *Señora* Augusto purchased most of the roll for her son's upcoming nuptials. As she was impatiently browsing through the fashion magazines that were scattered on the counter, I climbed the ladder, took down the fabric and lay it on the cutting table. There were only about 4 meters of beauty left in the fabric. I suggested that she buy all of it, but she, with much pettiness, insisted on only two and a half meters, which would leave me a piece of fabric that would only be enough for a vest. The aroma of cooking beans filled the store. I placed the fabric on the measuring table, measured twice, took the scissors and started cutting.

"Good morning *Señora* Augusto." My big sister Celeste's voice could be heard from the stairs. "I asked *Señor* Mudja for more colors from that nice silk. How are you enjoying the sewing?"

"The fabric is of superb quality; that is why I came to buy some more. Only it's terribly expensive," said the *Señora* and walked around the store feeling other fabrics. Celeste stood behind me and whispered, "It's crooked; let me."

I stopped to place the scissors on the table because everyone knows that you do not hand over scissors from one hand to another, but Celeste snatched them from my hand and placed her fingers in the scissors. "What are you doing?" I hissed in anger.

Señora Augusto noticed the switch and clicked her tongue. My ears and cheeks turned red. I knew little Celeste was right, it was crooked, but it was the first time scissors passed from hand to hand like that, and I hated her for making me do it. I also disliked *Señora* Ivona Augusto. No blouse would come out of that fabric for me. I wanted to run home, but little Celeste ordered me, "Stay! There's a lot of work today."

I spent the whole day with her at the store, looking for signs that something terrible that was about to happen. The day ended, and we didn't fight. I almost forgot about the scissors fiasco. But then Napoleon started to feel sick. He came back from his evening stroll pale and quiet. He didn't jump out of his stroller but was carried in by my father, who met my mother outside and was seated at the table. The smell of the meatballs and the *fagiolini* was tantalizing, but uncharacteristically, he didn't want to eat. Mother forced him, since she believed he was acting up. Aunt Celeste interfered as usual: "Leave him."

But Mother insisted. Napoleon ate a little and then vomited it all up. Mother placed her lips on his forehead and panicked. He was burning up. I couldn't stop thinking about the scissors, but didn't say a word.

Father gave instructions to everyone and set out to look for *Dottore* Maroccetti. A great deal of luck was required to find the doctor at his home in January. *Dottore* Maroccetti would be in the nearby towns taking care of the winter casualties. Only those with personal ties to him were able to get hold of him. At dawn, Dad came back with the doctor, holding his black briefcase that smelled like medicine, his pink hands fiddling his gray goatee and his silver watch that dangled from his eternal brown vest.

The doctor's serious look rested on my dad's liquor cabinet when he left the room after examining Napoleon. He prescribed medicine and gave them to older Celeste, who took the prescription with shaking hands, and he and my dad closed off in the kitchen for a hushed conversation.

During that week, *Dottore* Maroccetti came every morning to visit. In the first couple of days, he stayed a little to have a shot of *grappa* together with Alfredo. Later on, he would just enter for a quick visit to check Napoleon, who was getting smaller and smaller under the duvet on my parent's bed. His serious look did not change. After three days, he recommended to stop the medication and try to break the fever with vinegar-soaked washcloths.

For two weeks, the smell of chicken broth infused with fear hung in the air. During the first few days, older Celeste would still argue with my mother. After that, heavy silence, like brokered—Deep blue.

At night, we all stayed up, placing cold compresses on Napoleon's pale forehead. He would open his eyes, breathe heavily, and throw up every once in a while. I tried to tell him funny stories, but he became introverted and didn't respond anymore.

Dottore Maroccetti's visits grew shorter. Little Celeste and I didn't exchange words, but we were both thinking about the scissors. At the end of the first week, two more pairs of scissors were tied to the table. I never cut fabric again.

Toward the end, after pink *Dottore* Maroccetti, with his piercing hands and desperate looks, shut himself together with Dad in the kitchen, little Celeste and I pinned our ears to the door trying to figure out what was being said. It wasn't established whether it was tuberculosis or pneumonia, but it was clear that a calamity had befallen us. The doctor refused to accept the money that Dad offered him, nor the drink. We girls were forbidden from entering our parents' bedroom. Heavy silence fell on our home. Mother would leave the room when Celeste entered and cry. Her cry was profound and scary.

Dad blamed *Dottore* Maroccetti, and I couldn't bring myself to tell him about the scissors. I prayed to God, the only prayer I knew by heart, "*Shma Israel*" (Listen, Israel[1]). I heard my parents mumbling prayers, too. It didn't help. Napoleon passed away. He died. At noon, I returned from school to a deafening silence. The storefront's shutter was half pulled down. For a moment, I hoped that they took him to a hospital in Milan. I bent down and entered the store to see little Celeste sitting on the floor in the dark—*morto*.

Napoleon was my first death and my only brother.

---

1   *Shma Israel*—A Hebrew prayer that is perceived as the most basic declaration of faith in the Jewish religion.

"Morto"
(Dead)

I will carry the look on my mother's face the day Napoleon died until the day I die.

Those days, I promised myself I would never have children, out of the fear of loss. My father, who liked his daughters but was hanging on to the hope he would produce more sons, kept jumping from bed to bed of the town's women, seeking comfort.

I wasn't allowed to attend the funeral. After the funeral, the shop closed for a week, and hundreds of people flocked to our house. Mother sat in the living room with a hollow gaze on her face, still reeking of chicken soup. Dad paid Vercelli's rabbi to come and pray with him, and we had to keep the silence and prepare food together with older Celeste, who invaded my mother's kitchen kingdom. Little Celeste, who by the age of seventeen already knew how to cook better than our aunt, oversaw the task. And so we were closed off in the kitchen, while in the living room, Jews and neighbors from all around were coming and going.

Dottore Maroccetti came every night looking at me with investigative stares each time I walked into the room, carrying trays of *marzipan*, which we had prepared from almonds that were ground before the guests arrived to prevent the noise, and ladyfingers baked with nuts and vanilla sticks. We also served coffee and *grappa*. I knew he wanted me to marry his pink son even though he wasn't Jewish.

We didn't go to school for the whole week. When the *Shiva*[2] ended, Mother packed two boxes with Napoleon's clothes and toys in a tearful silence and gave them to the rabbi to hand out to the needy. No memory was left of Napoleon, apart from his little pillow, which Mother would hug every night when she laid in her bed. Every day for a month, Mother would visit the little pile of rocks erected in memoriam at the cemetery, and one time agreed to take me with her. This was my first visit to the cemetery. I visited her father's tombstone, her mother's, and on the wall, next to the most important people of Vercelli and the children, Napoleon was buried. We didn't talk about death. No one spoke of Napoleon. Only a pillow, memories, and a heavy discomfort that led nowhere remained.

After Napoleon passed away, I believed I would never marry. I would not have to polish shoes, watch the tomatoes so they didn't overripe, or bend over the stove to check the *biscotti*, and wouldn't have to lose any children.

When I grew up, I would wake up each morning, dress in my finest clothes, meet interesting people, and eat what others had cooked, and would not risk loss. I already knew then that I would never be this great aunt that lives with her brother and his family. I did not have a brother anymore.

---

2   Jewish mourning period of seven days.

They said I looked like my father. The wide nose and the dark shining eyes came from him. From Mother, I received the hips, black hair, and her smile.

Some say there is another woman in Vercelli that has my dad's smile and our eyes. They told me about her a few years ago, and I even thought once to investigate the matter but gave up on the idea. I can surely believe that, in Vercelli and its surroundings, there are strangers walking around carrying our genes, but it doesn't matter anymore. Alfredo lusted over other women but loved Anneta. He would spend hours trying to comfort her, wiping her tears. He kept on blaming the doctor. She was haunted by her conscience until the day she died. Napoleon's death changed our family. Alfredo, my father, lost his joy for life and spent less time with us.

In the first month, whenever I entered a shop or a place with other people, it became silent and people would stare at me. At school, I managed to gain attention even from girls who did not relate to me before. It created a situation in which I was invited to more birthdays and gatherings, and I was even asked to come to the field behind the cemetery.

Long-faced, blond Claudia; Sara, her thick-skinned, bushy-eyebrowed friend; and brown Leona, who was never noticed but was always with them, circled me at the first recess. It was the first time I noticed Leona's kind eyes and listened to their conversation. So far, they were an uninviting, tight group. Napoleon's death, my week-long absence—and upon my return, the announcement in front of the whole class that I had returned to school and that everyone shared my grief—while I was turning red, caused Claudia, upon whom all transpired, to invite me.

I nodded "yes" as I was biting into my *pesto* sandwich, fearing that I had something in my teeth, and remained seated in my place. In the second recess, I stepped outside, trying to ease my pounding heart. What was in that field? What would I be asked to do? How much would my mother worry when I was late to return home? On the other hand, I couldn't refuse them.

As we left school, I, with my simple dress, cotton socks, and worn-out shoes, accompanied this group of girls with their layered dresses and their matching lace stockings to the rice field closest to the cemetery.

We sat under a tree in a spot where no one could see us on a scarf that Claudia placed on the ground. Up close, I was able to see that on the lacy, layered dress, she had stains, near the knees. From a distance, I could see the cemetery, and they noticed I could as well. The cemetery was desolate.

They sat in a circle, chatting about the lesson, and every once in a while, looked at me. I was glad they had something to talk about, and I needed to say nothing, and so I kept quiet. I tried to figure out how long this would take, as I couldn't stop thinking about Anneta and the dinner that awaited me at home.

I noticed Claudia pulling out her big sister's lipstick and a mirror from her bag, and they started applying the lipstick on one another. I was the only Jewish girl in the circle, so when my turn came up, I told them that we were not allowed, during the first month of mourning, to doll up or wear makeup. They looked at each other, and then Claudia started telling a story about her big sister that has a boyfriend, mimicking busty Laura and her boyfriend Francesco's kissing and moaning noises.

My head started spinning, both from the heat and the stress and hunger. Suddenly, they looked ridiculous to me, with their pinkish-purple lipstick adorning their faces. I was nauseous as I felt the *pesto* coming up. From afar, the cemetery was looking at me.

I got up. "You are pale," said Leona.

"Yes, I am not feeling so well," I said, trying to remove the leaves from my socks and dress. "I also think that my mom will worry, as I always go home straight after school."

Suddenly, I felt sorry for my mother. For half an hour, she had already been waiting, together with feeling orphaned from my brother and miserable—like someone who couldn't wear lipstick.

"Thank you for inviting me. It was very kind of you. I would love to come again," I said as I grabbed my bag in front of their startled faces and started running. After about two hundred meters, when the tree was far away and all I could see were figures, I stopped and vomited the *pesto* sandwich.

I arrived with a pale face to a closed-off, quiet home. My mother was in bed taking her afternoon nap, and no one noticed I had entered. I washed my face and climbed into bed as well. My mother's cool hand on my forehead woke me up.

I didn't go to school for another whole week, as I fell ill with such a bad flu that even my sister Celeste brewed me tea and changed the cold compresses on my forehead. The girls from class took turns preparing my homework, all the while enjoying Anneta's delicacies.

I didn't leave the room and asked my father not to call the doctor. I felt I would be all right. Everyone around me was very worried. I must have had a very high fever when I was ill, as I kept seeing in front of me the girls with their lipstick, and each time anew, this sight gave me chills, causing me to vomit. Since then, I haven't touched *pesto*.

When I went back to school a week later, I was thinner, and the rumors about Anneta's delicacies had spread. I was escorted to my seat in the classroom by many looks of appreciation. I was never invited again by Claudia's posse to the rice fields next to the cemetery, but they did greet me hello.

Mother never made chicken soup again, but she still loved pampering us. She entered the kitchen and almost never came out. The thick aroma of her cuisine went with us into every corner, sticking to our skin, to the walls and to the glowing rolls of fabric in the shop. Smells of frying goose liver, pizza, *gnocchi* and a roast made with red wine and caramelized onions. Delicacies were always abundant and sometimes shared with the neighbors. If Alfredo didn't come home, she would save a plate for him, and even when we ate, although Napoleon's chair stayed empty, he was forever present in our memory.

Napoleon's death appeased the animosity between my big sister Celeste and me a little. We had some kind of "sisterhood" as we both lost our brother. A death of a brother in the family casts shame on it. It was terrible to witness the grief and live with the loss. We all felt sorry for Anneta and Alfredo.

Once in a while, I recalled Claudia mimicking the voices

her sister and boyfriend made and tried to listen if I could hear voices like that coming from my parents' bedroom, but it was always very quiet.

During meal times, in order to ease the silence, we would tell what happened in the store. Mother never said anything, and Father was always sad. We would plan, in advance, what we would talk about. When there was nothing to tell, Celeste riddled me in math as Anneta and Alfredo raised their heads waiting for me to answer. I always knew the answers to any kind of math exercise.

As the days passed, the meals became tastier. Mother really invested herself in dishes like *ravioli* filled with fresh artichokes and topped with sage sauce—a dish that took almost an entire day to prepare. Celeste was always at her side, peeling the thorns off the artichokes, blanching the sage.

We all puffed up as time went by.

Since Napoleon's death, every time my mother lifted her eyes from the pots, I could see the pain. In my father's eyes, I could see disappointment, sadness, and restlessness.

From my great Aunt Celeste, I inherited the ability to understand things before they were explained to me. I had some sort of inner sense. My mother hated her observation skills, as my aunt would diagnose her to her face as well as behind her back. According to the smells, Celeste could tell the mood Anneta was in—sad, very sad, or depressed. Looking at what she wore, she could tell whether she went out or not. But worse than that, something in my aunt's piercing looks told her whether Alfredo was coming home or not. When he didn't come home for several days, she would hiss, "He's coming back on…" and it was almost always true.

She wasn't a mother or someone's wife, but she could read every customer that walked into the store, categorize her according to education, happiness, and her romantic situation. She could also tell the second a customer walked in whether it would be a good sale or not. There were situations in which she wouldn't even put down the paper she was reading. This ability of hers to understand reality, to see beyond, hear past the spoken words was the common denominator my aunt Celeste and I shared. My big sister did not have this ability or if she did, she never listened to it. Accompanying all that were many superstitions that helped us connect with good fortune. I didn't think Celeste was a witch, nor was she one, but there were certain rules she was meticulous about, which I made sure to keep my whole life as well, such as: do not pass a knife from one hand to another, nor salt or scissors. In fact, I hate scissors. On the other hand, numbers, I love. I discovered the world of numbers during that cursed winter in the store. Alfredo realized that, too, and every night, he would sit with me to do the books.

Milano
(A Trip to Milan)

In the evening, when the dinner dishes had been washed, and the scent from the *macchinetta* was rising through the air, we would count our daily revenues. We used to bet by midday about how much revenue we would have at the end; some days we got it right.

Dad would settle in his chair with a glass of *grappa* in his hand and money that went from one hand to the other. Some bills were stashed in Mom's colorful tin can that she kept in our Passover dish cabinet.

This was the time to make plans for the future. Travels, purchases, needs, wants, and fantasies—it was all discussed around the dinner table on full stomachs and a full piggy bank. My father and Aunt Celeste were discussing a trip to Milan and about little Celeste—a death in the family reduced the chance of an appropriate match for her.

"He's from Milan, a lawyer, educated, and he also has an apartment in a great location in Milan," Aunt Celeste told my sister.

Little Celeste graduated her studies with honors and was polite and presentable. Our relationship wasn't close, as could be expected of sisters who shared a room and a closet. I rejoiced in her upcoming departure, as her bed faced the window, and I would have more room in the closet. I also felt sorry for her. She was about to marry a stranger, whom she met only three times. But she was cooperative, and sometimes, it seemed she was happy to distance herself from Lina and me and from the grief that somehow always filled the air at home.

I asked her, "Is he nice?"

"He looks fine. Mother says that couples learn to live together, and I see it as a good opportunity for me to have a life of my own. You will have to learn to peel artichokes now."

Her thoughts of "They won't be able to borrow my clothes" and "I will not have to see them hug now" she kept to herself and continued to fiddle with her embroidery in her typical cold demeanor. It looked like she wasn't at all fearful of what was ahead of her, and even if she was, she had no intention of sharing her thoughts with me.

The details were finalized, and all that was left to do was set the date. Should the marriage between little Celeste and a rich lawyer from Milan take place within the year's mourning period, it would indicate that the Bosola family had beaten death, and if they took place after a year, it would leave time to prepare a proper dowry. Eventually, the date was set for ten months after Napoleon passed away.

Preparations started immediately at home and in the store. My sister nodded with indifference at the sight of the linen fabrics chosen for her. She reacted in the same manner when the linen was embroidered, the towels sewn and the lists made.

A lot was happening in front of the large mirror: ongoing fittings of lacy undergarments, taffeta skirts, and silk vests. I hoped during this time for moments of closeness between us, but Celeste stayed distant and only blushed each time Guido's name was mentioned.

Right before my big sister was about to leave the house, I got my period. The intensity of the pain took me by surprise. I asked Celeste why she withheld the agony from me. She answered that pain is a mental state, that she didn't experience pain, and that I was spoiled. Condescending Celeste, the smart, never-got-caught-cutting-a-crooked-piece-of-cloth Celeste, never left pasta residue on any pot or quickly licked sauce from her finger. "Perfect Celeste" we called her behind her back. Despite her indifference, she was my sister.

"They are not short on money over there," older Celeste declared.

"His money doesn't impress me; I'll try not to spend," my sister replied. "We will live on a side street, and I will find my way to the market and the butcher. I plan to cook and organize my own home."

I pictured her filling bottles of tomato sauce in the summer, collecting every drop.

"We will come visit you," I promised and imagined how Lina and I would enter into her perfectly clean and tidy living room, filled with treasures from the market in Milan.

"You will come when I invite you," she replied.

Hours after the modest wedding (within the mourning year), Guido and his young bride vanished into the horizon. We met quite a lot on the weekends, and the distance helped us grow closer.

It wasn't but a few short months later, that the happy announcement came. Alfredo was about to become a grandfather. He walked around proudly and started cooperating with the lawyer that had just joined the family. Real estate was bought and sold with the help of Guido's shrewd contracts.

We grew to like him. On one of our visits over there, we three sisters walked around the Milan market. Toward evening, we said good-bye to Celeste, who went home, and we proceeded to the train station.

We took our time.

Lina and I wandered around the alleys of Milan admiring the buildings, shops, and shop windows. When we reached the train station, we saw our train departing from the platform. As it turned out, it was the last train for the day, and the next train wasn't leaving before morning.

We didn't regret it. Now, so we discussed, Celeste, our sister, would have to put us up for the night and add us to her dinner table.

We reached her home an hour later. Giggling, we knocked on her door, only to find her and Guido in the midst of dinner. He opened the door to us as she sat in a pale-blue robe across from him at the table. On the table, we saw lemon scaloppini and potatoes. A delightful familiar aroma filled the room, but there were only two portions of this fine cuisine on the table. For us, she made pasta, and they both hosted us with silence. Lina and I cuddled on the sofa for the night's sleep, and Lina nicknamed them "The Dry Ones," a nickname that stuck with them forever.

Biella

Business was booming at the store. Lina measured and cut the fabrics, and I was in charge of accounting. One night, after we were almost done paying for the wedding, which was modest yet dignified, Father said to me with a smile on his face, "Now we are saving for you."

"I want to choose my own husband," I said to him and to older Celeste. They looked at one another and smiled.

At the market, I was always staring at the older women, those where something inside them had died, sitting at a stall—with a husband the kind of which you would not shine their shoes—always wearing the same worn-out dress, fat and defeated.

They reminded me of my mother. She, too, was dead inside. Although she wasn't a peddler in the market but had status and a home, her downfall started after Napoleon died.

There is nothing like a nice wedding to maintain the family's name and happiness. But she wore only black, and in Celeste's wedding, she stood out with her unflattering modest black attire. It seemed like she was happy for Celeste, but her smiles were a bit askew. Compared to her, Alfredo wore his new suit, pouring drinks for everyone and smiling.

The aroma of peppers and garlic accompanied me into the

kitchen. Anetta talked to me without lifting her head from the pots. "There is someone they are thinking of fixing you up with. He is the son of the butcher from across the road. They are Jewish, too, a good family. You will be well provided for. He's a little older than you, and the mother is very nice."

I knew short, chubby Luigi. He always shyly smiled at me when we ran into each other. A good guy, but the thought of the smell that stuck to his skin gave me the chills. "They will not decide for me!" I cried out.

"I had an arranged marriage, and it worked out fine. Your father is truly the love of my life, so don't think you know it all."

But I knew... I knew that with the son of the butcher, his smell, and his pockmarked face, I was not getting married. I knew I would leave Vercelli. I knew I would choose for myself.

At dinner, over the *gnocchi* plate, my father surprised me, "Tomorrow, I am going out of town. I heard you had plans. Come join me, see what's going on outside the town..." Older Celeste made a face, Lina poked around her plate with a gloomy face and my mother, Anetta, kept silent.

More than I wanted to leave, I wanted not to stay. "If I go, you are coming with me," I whispered to Lina before we went to bed.

"In any case, you can't choose whom to marry," Lina said in her smart voice.

"I can," I answered determinately.

The next day, we arose early to catch the train to Biella. We were headed to the Vitale, a thriving textile factory. *Señor* Samuelle was the first Jew who dared to open a business outside the ghetto walls on the town's main street. He was the first born of a large family and took it upon himself to provide for his mother and his eight brothers and sisters. He married Josephina at the ripe age of thirty-eight, and they had four sons: Maurizio, Alberto, Emanuelle, and Michelangelo—the princes of the House of Vitale.

The family's house stood right at the exit from the train station, across from the only gas station in town. I recognized it from the descriptions that reached our town square and were whispered jealously. It was a five-story covered building, and on each floor, there were covered balconies with shining wooden railings. Among its walls, hid a vegetable garden and a pond with goldfish, next to which the aunties gathered in the afternoon.

We walked side by side without talking. We were a father and daughter who knew the way. Parked at the entrance to the large textile factory were a couple of shining white and light-blue Fiat cars. The guard smiled a toothless smile at us out of a dark room. We were welcomed by the smell of gas fumes, dust, and cotton.

We walked past the guard and sat in the waiting room. Dozens of workers walked by as they entered the factory, all dressed in blue work overalls, and the women had their hair bundled in head kerchiefs. I was cold, and it felt like the inside of a hive. Each time the door opened, the hustle and bustle of the machines and the workers could be heard.

My blue dress, which I ironed the previous evening with the store's iron, was already wrinkled up. The braids I made in my hair were unraveling. I felt awkward putting lipstick on, so I felt quite pale. On top of it all, I was wearing a pretty, new pair of shoes that gave my legs a longer than usual look but were hurting me terribly. I wore a nice bra that made me look like a woman or so I felt it did.

At 10 a.m. sharp, he stood at the door. Maurizio Vitale was tall and emitted the manly scent of cigarettes and soap.

"*Per favore*," he said with a cigarette in his mouth. With one hand, he opened the warehouse door, and with the other, signaled us to follow him. We walked through giant halls bustling with activity and entered the cutting room. In the center of the room, stood five cutting tables much larger than ours, and around them, mountains of colorful rolls of fabric, walls of them.

Workers wearing blue uniforms showed us the merchandise, and Alfredo meticulously picked up whatever we needed. I stood at his side, overwhelmed by the abundance. The smells, colors and sounds confused my senses. Trying to keep up the pace, I carefully wrote down our detailed order. Maurizio stood leaning against the entrance door. With my back to him, I could feel his piercing gaze.

I turned for a second to take a quick look at him, and our eyes met. He smiled. The sunrays that turned the dust twirling in the air goldlit up his shirt, which glittered in white in the midst of all the colors around. The world was silent. Within all the commotion, all I could hear were the puffs from his cigarette, and when he threw it on the ground, stepping on it, the soles of his shoes. He bent over to pick up the cigarette butt he stepped on, and I felt my cheeks burning. I knew my dress was too simple.

We completed an order for 15,000 *lirettas*.

"*Besta cuzi*," I said to Alfredo as he sat heavily on a chair next to one of the cutting tables.

Maurizio advanced toward the table where the rolls piled up. "How old are you?" He turned to me.

Alfredo stood up. "She's nearly eighteen, and she calculates faster than me."

Maurizio and Alfredo discussed payment. Suddenly, I felt tired and sat down in place of Alfredo. Maurizio's clean smell cramped my stomach. "She's eighteen." The words echoed in my ears as my face turned red again.

"I'll give you a fifteen percent discount because Sergio sent you," Maurizio concluded and looked straight at me. "The goods will be shipped to you within a few days. Come with me."

He held my notes. "Nice handwriting," he said to Alfredo while walking. He hastened his stride and pulled out the packet of cigarettes from his pocket. We climbed the noisy iron stairs after him. From above, the empire looked even bigger. The smell of gasoline and cotton in the air caused Alfredo to cough, although it didn't prevent him from accepting the cigarette Maurizio offered.

Lina and I once sneaked a cigarette. Lina coughed terribly, but I loved it. For a minute there, I could imagine myself between them, holding a long cigarette holder, but they never offered. In order to light Alfredo's cigarette, Maurizio handed me the notebook. The palm of his hand flickered on my fingers, taking my breath away. We stood there in silence in front of a closed door until they finished their cigarettes.

Maurizio knocked on the door and opened it. Behind a desk piled with samples of wool and fabrics, sat Mr. Samuelle, dressed in a blue woolen suit and a fancy silk tie. I was surprised to see how short he was when he stood up to shake our hands. "*Señor* Basola, and Miss..."

"Vittoria," I replied, flushed.

"Welcome. Sergio told me about you," he said. His mustache was impressive, more than Maurizio's, and his eyes were wise and piercing. His physique was firm and sturdy, and he moved with a surprising lightness. The men sat in the drawing corner, staring at me. My dress was threaded, my feet were sore, and my cheeks were burning. My cheeks turned even redder as I asked in a whisper where the restroom was. Samuelle's secretary escorted me there. The scent of soap—the same one that came from Maurizio—a shining toilet bowl and the golden faucet in the sink astonished me. I lengthened my stay in the fancy restroom, trying to come to my senses.

When I returned to the office, I found Alfredo and *Señor* Samuelle having a drink and talking in a friendly manner. Throughout the years, I tried to recall what they were talking about without success. Only the smell of alcohol and cigarette smoke remained etched in my brain.

At home, Lina welcomed me with a ton of questions. I extended my arm that still smelled of soap, "Smell this."

"Did you buy soap?" she asked.

"No," I answered. "We bought loads of fabric, but this smell was the most spectacular of all."

From the moment I returned home, all I wished for was to go back to Biella. I forgot about my fears of the death of a child for a while, couldn't see the disadvantages of a relation-ship, all I wanted was Biella. It smelled like blossoms and had fancy shop window displays. Elegant women in pleated skirts with lace parasols roamed its streets. I wanted to be like them; I wanted exactly what they had. I yearned to smell the sweet scent of Maurizio's soap, shine his shoes, prepare meals for him, and to hold him. I felt something in me change. I asked my mother how someone could tell about love.

She answered tiredly, "Love isn't told, it's learned, with time."

The next morning at the cemetery, at Napoleon's grave, I whispered to him that I may have found a clue to the age-old question of what love is, and asked his help in making my hopes come true.

L'Amore
(Love)

Unlike Celeste, whose arranged marriage and wedding consisted of an array of errands everyone managed to the best of their ability—one in which only once in a while, she gave a little smile—I wasn't embarrassed by the talk about love. Shame did not flourish in me. Some inner voice within me confirmed the legitimate pleasant sensations throughout my body. At night, I dreamt about Maurizio, and during the days, I daydreamed about the very same thing. I tried to recreate the feeling in my stomach, the weakness in my arms, and thinking about Maurizio did just that. When the merchandise arrived at the store, I cordially placed it on the shelves, finding myself trying not to sell it so we would have something left from the visit.

I was afraid he wouldn't want to marry me. I talked to older Celeste about my concerns that we were not wealthy enough to marry into such a family, that we came from different classes. Celeste looked at me from the top of the ladder she was standing on in the store, lay down the blue fabric, and said, "Your father says that they have the money and we have the sacks to put it in. You are beautiful and smart, and you will marry whomever your father tells you to marry..."

I replied that I already knew who I wanted to marry. Celeste climbed heavily down the ladder, stared at me, and said, "What has to happen will happen."

I knew that her name was written all over this matchmaking deal. She knew *Señora* Vitale's brother. She passed the message along. I also caught the whispers between her and Alfredo. He, too, was concerned about marrying into such a rich family, and I was aware that despite all his complaining about us girls—that we were confusing his brains and squeezing his pockets dry—he didn't really want me to leave home.

Life went on. Maurizio and his mother were invited to visit Vercelli and to come to us for dinner. Dishes that had been stashed away for a while were taken out to air. Anetta didn't send me to the market, but went to choose the zucchini, *filetto*, and *pomodoro*, as well as pick the basil from the greengrocer's garden by herself.

The eggs for the *Zabaglione* were already resting on the counter on the morning of the dinner, and Alfredo was sent to buy the appropriate liquor, wine and of course petit fours that Anetta forgot to serve.

Lina and I were entrusted to clean the house and to set the table. Alfredo stopped by for lunch, bringing the beverages, and vanished. Older Celeste was in the store, and the house was filled with the aroma of *gnocchi*, *fagiolini*, potatoes and almond cake.

I debated whether to wear the light-blue dress or the cream, pleated skirt with a green shirt. Lina and I went through my entire closet, and eventually, I wore a floral dress, which was less flattering, but in which I could help my mother take out the food from the kitchen.

They arrived in a light-blue car that blocked the entire street.

Out of the car, came *Señora* Josephina wearing white lacquered shoes and a light-blue suit. At her side was Maurizio, all smelling of pleasant soap wearing a light-blue shirt that hung loosely on him.

Lina welcomed them downstairs, and they all went up to the first floor. The sound of the store's shutter could be heard as we all welcomed them as well.

"You are very pretty," said Josephina, as her eyes rested on Lina, with her golden curls and shining face.

Maurizio smiled at me. His smile reassured my thoughts about the fact that she didn't say anything to me; in fact, she didn't give me a second look.

"Samuelle had to stay," he told me. I was sorry about that. *Señor* Samuelle seemed very nice, which made me think that maybe they only came to fulfill an obligation.

Maurizio sat down in Alfredo's chair, who hurried to offer him a drink. He politely refused and replied he'd much rather drink soda water. Alfredo poured himself another drink, handed him a tall glass of soda water, sat in front of him and they both talked.

Señora Josephina also refused a drink and sat upright and uneasy on the extra chair that was placed opposite the sofas. The home I loved so much with my mom's and Celeste's crochet tablecloths seemed tedious and sad in the face of her white lacquered shoes and the starchy light-blue of her suit.

Her black eyes examined every item.

Napoleon's photo was also gazing at us from the sideboard, and I could see Josephina checking it as well.

We had a death in the family from typhus or pneumonia; Mr. Samuelle didn't come—many bad omens.

I walked into the kitchen. The *gnocchi* floated around in the pasta pot, and Anetta was fishing them out one by one and placing them in the tomato sauce that had shining basil leaves floating in it. This was the first dish that Maurizio finished. He pecked at the *antipasti*.

Alfredo opened a bottle of wine with the *gnocchi*. *Señora* Josephina took a careful sip, and when she tasted the *gnocchi*, she lifted her eyes and said, "Very classy."

Maurizio smiled at me again. His smile washed over the room, and the house seemed to give a sigh of relief.

The chill dissipated, the food was served, the smells refined, and I only concentrated on Maurizio. My mother's delicacies were passing through his mustache, and it looked like he was enjoying himself more with every passing minute. I felt proud and frightened at the same time. There was no way I would ever learn to cook like that.

After dinner, the moist almond cake was served, and Maurizio and I went for a walk. The streets of Vercelli glowed in my honor, Maurizio held my waist, and I needed nothing more.

"Dinner was very good," said Maurizio as we sat on the bench in front of the *piazza*. People passing by looked at me, sitting with a handsome, thin guy in a light-blue shirt.

Amused he continued, "Two months ago, I went with my

mother to visit a Jewish family from Genoa. We were asked to dinner. I noticed the chicken feathers in the soup, and later, said I wasn't feeling well. I couldn't keep on eating."

I was happy to hear that he went there with only his mother, too, and for a moment I was proud and thankful for my mom and her cooking.

"I can't cook like that," I hurried to blurt out.

"Don't worry," said Maurizio. "I liked you even before I knew whether you could cook or not, and you can always learn. Let's head back before my mother scares them even more."

During our stroll, *Señora* Josephina sat with my aunt discussing art studies, the store and a little about Mussolini's Jewish mistress, whom my Aunt Celeste knew and used to brag about. Lina remained there only to tell me that Anetta listened to their conversation sitting in the lounge, and Alfredo stood at the window.

Whether it was the food, my aunt, the *Shma Israel*, or the fact that God elected to take Napoleon, the wedding date was set after that visit.

We met twice more before the wedding, and on both occasions, we talked at length. He told me about his brothers, his family and his passion for scenery and hikes. I nodded and told him a little about Vercelli and my mother's cooking. We both loved to eat, and it was clear to me that we could go on talking forever.

I tried to be attentive, but most of the time, I nodded in agreement, savoring the scent of soap and cigarettes without getting to the bottom of things. I told him I liked working, implying that it was something I wanted to continue doing as a married woman. Maurizio got serious, pondered my words, and said that there was enough work for everyone. He also said I had better learn how to make *Zabaglione* like my mother. I longed to have him close, attracted to his scent, and dreamt about a passionate kiss like in the movies, but was scared that Alfredo would catch us red-handed and cancel the wedding.

I was possessed with passion and fear. I negotiated with God, saying that after losing Napoleon, I was entitled to all this happiness. When happiness came, I was shocked by its intensity. I wanted Maurizio to yearn for me, and when he did, I was scared of its fortitude. I also panicked from the fact that I would have the wedding dress and shoes I always dreamed about.

Toward the gathering of the families before the wedding, I prayed that Lina would fancy Emanuelle, Maurizio's younger brother. On the day before the gathering, I told Lina about him and asked Maurizio to do the same with his brother. Lina was considered beautiful, and obviously, would have no trouble finding a groom, but I wanted her close to me, so I hoped with all my heart that Emanuelle would fall in love with her.

During the gathering, it was hard to ignore him looking at her, and she blushed each time he addressed her. Maurizio and I now had something more to talk about, and from the heights of our love, we started dating in a foursome.

Matrimonio
(A Wedding)

The beautiful street in Vercelli and the joy around us was depicted in our wedding photos well. But what wasn't seen in the pictures was *Señora* Vitale's condescending demeanor, the fact that we were not good enough for her. The pictures couldn't show my sorrow at leaving my mother, my beloved Lina, and the tastes and smells of home. They didn't show my fear of the new, the unknown, and of Maurizio's mustache that could feel nice but might also scratch.

On the day of the wedding, I woke up from a dream about meeting Napoleon. I wanted to share the joy of my wedding with him, but he ran away. The aroma from the *crostini* and piping hot coffee filled the house. Alfredo was pacing in the kitchen like a caged lion. Introverted Anetta wiped her tears and cuddled me with warm hugs. I asked her if she would join me when I visited the cemetery, but she preferred to stay in the kitchen, making the deserts, and not visit the cemetery on a wedding day. "It's unlucky," she said.

I had to leave the house and be by myself for a while. I went to the cemetery to say good-bye to Napoleon and stood there in front of the wall that had the names of my grandparents, whom I didn't know, engraved on them. I told Napoleon that I was about to marry Maurizio, the man I picked out for myself. I promised that I would come and visit my parents, and asked him to pray with me that Lina would also come to Biella. It was even closer than Milan.

The leaves on the ground of the cemetery twirled, the skies grew darker, and I felt dazed. Walking away for the last time as a girl, I bid my childhood farewell.

Waiting for me at home, was Lina, in a pink silk dress and combed curls. She drew a bath for me, and while the perfumed waters caressed my naked body, I blushed, knowing that the next time I would take off my clothes, Maurizio would be looking at me with lusting eyes. Lina brushed my hair and styled it into a fancy hairdo. We laughed and cried as she helped me button the tiny pearl buttons on the back of my silk gown. I left the room I grew up in for the last time, gazing at the large mirror that held all my childhood memories within.

The scent of lilies and cinnamon pastry hung in the air of the living room and made me dizzy. My waist was tightened by a corset, and I could hardly breathe. Lina pranced behind me holding my bouquet.

Maurizio's family waited for us in the synagogue. Josephina, wearing a cream-colored suit, pecked my cheek with a rigid and serious kiss. She didn't smile at me, not even on my wedding day.

My mother, dressed in a widely cut black dress, did not look as impressive as Mrs. Vitale, but her looks were loving and warm. I stayed by her side. *Señor* Samuelle hugged me warmly, and the Vitale brothers gave me cheerful kisses on both cheeks.

All the petit fours, the cakes and an array of delicacies my mother made rested on the tables at the reception. Mrs. Josephina didn't even consider taking off her white gloves. The guests, the cousins, and the brothers all tasted the food, and I felt like tasting it myself but could not allow it. The sugared pears looked at me, and I at them.

The smell of lilies filled the air in the synagogue. The sun came through the stained windows, and the synagogue, although worn out, was cozy and nice. The rabbi got up from the table, Lina gave me a glass of water, and Maurizio led me to the *Chuppa*. The commotion ceased immediately. My parents took me by the arms as I gazed at the faded carpet all the way there. I was aware of the uncomfortable new shoes I was wearing and tried not to trip.

My mother covered my face with the veil, and beyond the white cloth, everything seemed like a dream. I vaguely remember the taste of the wine; the sensation of the cold metal on my finger; the sound of breaking glass; the phrase, "If I shall forget thee, O Jerusalem…"; the flutter of Maurizio's lips on my face; and then I was a man's wife.

When the *Chuppa* ended, we all gathered in our home's living room, where sandwiches made by Anetta waited for us. I was unfortunately so busy collecting my things, I didn't get to eat. Anetta, befitting the mother of the bride, gave me two boxes with food for the road, kissed me on both my cheeks and wept. I cried, too. I sat with my uncomfortable shoes and dress next to the driver of the light-blue automobile that blocked the street.

Sposati
(Married)

After the wedding and the farewell hugs, I found myself blissful, frightened and teary-eyed, driving fast with my husband in the light-blue Fiat car, which was packed with luggage, toward our life together. Maurizio patted my thigh each time he changed gear and didn't stop humming songs the entire trip.

Maurizio didn't drink alcohol, not in the wedding nor ever. During his childhood, his nanny used to get him to sleep with alcohol, and he hated the smell of it, so he told me after the first meal together when my father was deeply hurt he did not join him for a drink.

Maurizio refused to live in the Vitale family big house with smiley *Señor* Samuelle and uptight Josephina. He rented a spacious well-lit apartment not far from the main house at *Via Trieste*. We arrived there early in the evening when the sun had just begun to set. I gave a quick look at my new home as Maurizio hurried to lead me into our bedroom. I sat on the edge of the armchair next to the canopy bed made up with starchy white linen. I took off my shoes and rubbed my aching feet. Maurizio leaned to me, grabbed my shoulders and started kissing me passionately. Everything happened so fast. I remember my wedding dress lying on the floor, his cool hands touching my body, in tune, knowingly. Without words, he taught me the magic of his body, the secrets of mine. The sensations and tastes were both strange and yet at the same time, familiar. Just like the scent of his body I had yearned for, for weeks. I closed my eyes and allowed him to perform his magic on my body.

I woke up the next day from a deep and dreamless slumber to the intoxicating smell of soap. Maurizio waited for me to prepare his coffee. He did not use loving nicknames, not for me nor for anyone else. From that morning until the last of his days, he called me "TO" instead of Vittoria. This was his way of telling me he loved me. The manner in which he pronounced my name and the way he looked at me.

We spent the first morning after the wedding with his parents. I couldn't bring myself to imagine rigid Josephina surrendering to *Señor* Samuelle's yearning touch.

Josephina made me feel ugly and inarticulate. She was aware of her effect on me and did nothing to change it. I didn't turn out to be an excellent housewife, and already in the first week of my marriage, I accompanied my husband to the factory every morning. He, for his part, kept his promise and allowed me to be a working wife.

Alfredo came to visit once a week, bringing baskets of groceries. Anetta's tomato sauce, *pesto*, and *Zabaglione* made Maurizio happy, and it was easier on me. Married life became a pleasant routine. Every evening after dinner, Maurizio submerged himself in the newspaper as I finished the accounting, and at 11 p.m., we shut off the lights together and loved each other.

The magic of our bed made me long in anticipation for nightfall. After our lovemaking, I would enter the washroom smiling at my blushing reflection with glittering eyes. Maurizio's presence made me more beautiful.

I knew my mother did not enjoy a man like mine. Maybe my father behaved like that with his occasional mistresses, but not with her. I dreaded the occasional mistress Maurizio might bring into my life, but he remained mine every night.

Maurizio was patient with me and kind, much more than with any other person in the world. I was the only one to know the kind of softness and pleasantness the man I married had.

Lina became my confidant. I could tell her about my love for Maurizio and our nights together, my work at the office, and my new life. I shared my new clothes with her and the joy of becoming "Mrs. Vitale," too. I told her everything in detail, as she waited for the time it would be her turn.

Gravidanza
(Pregnancy)

The pain in my breasts indicated to me I was pregnant. The doctor confirmed my feelings by ruling, "*Señora* Vitale, you better stop running around."

Maurizio was over the moon. The anticipation for a son made him love me even more. He lay for hours by my side, caressing my rounding body and sharing his dreams of our future together as a family. Throughout the pregnancy, I dreamt of Napoleon. Fears mixed together with hopes.

Bruno's labor was short and painful. Maurizio chose his name, and I was happy with his decision. Bruno was the first-born grandchild in the Vitale family. *Señor* Samuelle cried with excitement, and Josephina dressed up in a new suit and a hint of a smile. I felt like a winner, proud of myself, almost vain: I gave birth to a healthy baby boy, the first grandchild in the family.

My moments of glory were short-lived. After the circumcision ceremony, the house emptied from guests, and my body was hurting in places I never knew existed. My breasts were sore and bursting with milk, and I had dark circles under my eyes. Maurizio was ecstatic, but the passion and the heart-to-heart talks we used to have became a distant memory.

Bruno cried incessantly, and when I finally managed to get him to sleep, I unsuccessfully tried to be a housewife. I was intoxicated by the smell of my newborn baby and petrified of death.

Maurizio was in love with the concept of a family but did not lend much of a hand. I wished for my old life back. A week after delivery, I started smoking again. The cigarettes enabled me to escape from the constant crying and the smell of medicinal alcohol that filled the house. The cigarette allowed me to distance myself from home for a few minutes.

One afternoon, a few days after Bruno turned two months old, and after a couple of sleepless nights, Lina arrived to let me have a little break. Bruno woke up smiling, and I seized the opportunity to take a shower. I contemplated how I would manage to cook for Maurizio and welcome him home with a big smile. When I got out of the shower, Lina informed me that she was in a hurry to catch the train to Milan to surprise Celeste. She placed gurgling Bruno in his crib, kissed me and headed out. I restrained myself from bursting out crying. Heavy fatigue came over me, and all I wanted to do was sleep, but I had resolved to uphold my decision to cook Maurizio his favorite food.

I went into the kitchen.

The pile of dishes from the night before stared at me from the sink. I chopped tomatoes for the sauce, placed them in the only clean pot I could find, turned down the gas, and decided to climb into bed for a half-hour nap. Up until that day,

I never dared to go sleep when there was no one around to watch Bruno. When he slept for a few hours, I would deal with mountains of washing and dirty diapers.

Bruno was mumbling in the crib, which was placed in the hall, I put a pacifier in his mouth and went into the bedroom. I fell asleep immediately.

I dreamt of Napoleon. In my dream, he was playing with a rag doll I made for him, I could hear him laugh and saw him running and falling. I heard his cry. In my dream, he did not calm down, but cried and choked. I was sitting on a soft chair in the store, smelling the cooking tomatoes in Anetta's kitchen. I tried to get up to go to Napoleon, but my legs failed me.

Heavy banging on the door woke me up. For a minute, I thought I was still in the store in Vercelli. I jumped out of bed. My shirt was wet, and my hair was a mess. I smelled something burning, and Bruno was screaming.

I quickly picked Bruno up and made my way to the door through a smoke screen.

In front of me, stood Josephina, elegant as always, holding a tray of petit fours. She looked at me in shock. I opened my mouth, but no sound came out of it.

I turned my back to her, turned off the gas under the burnt pot, and headed to my bedroom, trying to soothe screaming Bruno. A reflection of a strange, ugly woman looked at me from the mirror. Tangled hair, red eyes, tracks of tears staining my face.

Josephina kept quiet. Without saying anything, she opened all the windows in the house. Bruno stopped crying, but the burnt smell was still in the air. I remained slumped on my bed. A few minutes later, Maurizio came home. I did not get up to welcome him. I was scared to put Bruno down, and I couldn't look my husband in the eye.

Maurizio came into the bedroom and gave me a smiling look. "Did Lina leave?" he asked compassionately. I did not answer him. My eyes filled with tears, my throat was blocked.

He took Bruno in his arms and left the room. I locked the door behind him. I stayed there for another long hour, agonizing about the near-disaster that was miraculously prevented. My breasts were sore and dripping, my stomach growling from hunger, and my head was pounding from panic and fatigue.

I knew that Maurizio and Josephine were talking about me in the next room. I knew I was to blame. I fell asleep with a pot on the stove and a baby in the hallway; the house could have been burnt down on both of us.

Maurizio knocked on the door: "TO? Is everything all right?" he asked in a soft voice. I said nothing. For the first time since we were married, a door was locked in our house.

"I will not let them take Bruno away from me," I mumbled.

"TO, open the door," Maurizio insisted.

"*Lacio starea*," ("Leave it") I answered in a squeaky voice. Leave.

At midnight, I opened the door. Maurizio was sitting in the kitchen wearing the same clothes he went to work in. Everything was cleaned and polished. Bruno was sleeping in the crib next to his father. I fell into Maurizio's arms sobbing. Maurizio stroked my head until I stopped crying, then lit a cigarette and handed it to me.

"*Tutto bene,*" he said. "Starting tomorrow, Armenia, the maid, will come every day. You will go back to work."

The petit fours were thrown in the dustbin, and the events of that night were never mentioned again. Armenia arrived every day, but many weeks passed before I calmed down and agreed to entrust Bruno to her care and return to work at the factory. I loved Bruno, but learned, not without difficulty, to accept the fact that motherhood did not come naturally for me.

In Eritrea
(Mussolini's War in Ethiopia)

Bruno turned six months old as Emanuelle and Lina's wedding date arrived.

Josephina had grown used to me, and just as I prayed, Emanuelle had fallen in love with my smiley, pleasant sister. She had become a part of the household at Josephina's home, and the pleated skirts that did not fit me anymore due to the pregnancy naturally passed on to her, and stayed with her, as well. Biella suited her, Emanuelle suited her, and so did being in love. Anetta, my mother, told me on my first visit to her after I got married that she believed that would happen. Lina, on her part, loved visiting me in Biella very much, and we dated in a foursome.

Their love was reflected in our love. We were the working adults, and they, the blonde and funny guy, would join us.

Lina excelled with her cooking in our kitchen, and Maurizio beamed each time she came for a visit. The four of us would sit down for dinner a few times a week, and as far as I was concerned, it was great.

I couldn't picture Lina joining me at work, but her presence in Biella was a blessing on my part, moreover since it helped my relationship with Josephina. Something in Lina's beauty caused Josephina to be nicer to me.

Emanuelle and Lina's wedding also took place in Vercelli. Anetta, crying over the fact that it was her last wedding, made her variety of delicacies. A few windows at the synagogue in Vercelli were cracked, but something about Lina's wedding was happier. The tension between the two families was no longer there, and I swear I could see Josephina smile.

When the draft orders for the war in Ethiopia came, Bruno was nine months old. Maurizio packed a bag and left, and Emanuelle did the same. There was no way for us to know what was happening to them over there. For fourteen months, only three letters arrived, and I kept thinking a calamity might happen. I missed Maurizio terribly. I missed our daily routine, our nights together, and his touch.

Armenia shared the days with me, sometimes even the nights. Very quickly, I had grown used to the fact I had a maid every day; the financial well-being gave me freedom. The vendors at the market used to call me "*Señora* Vitale." The country girl with the dead brother had vanished, and in her place was a married woman, a mother, a homeowner, and a working woman.

A heavy desk was placed in the office lobby, and seated at that desk, guided by *Señor* Vitale, I acquired the business accounting skills. Samuelle was in his sixties—a man of his generation, short and with a mustache. He managed his role as a father of the extended family with wisdom and pleasant-ry. He was proud of his loyalty to his homeland and proud to be a Jew. I saw a father and a teacher in him, and he found a listening partner in me and shared with me not only the secrets of running a business but also the intricate family web.

The relationship between my husband's parents and me grew tighter, and I had grown very fond of Alberto and Michelangelo, Maurizio's younger brothers, but nothing could calm my longing for Maurizio. I missed his loving looks, his yearning hands, and his complaining. The silence at the beginning and end of every day hurt my ears.

The letters informing us of the brothers' return from the war arrived two days before they did. They arrived at noon, wearing worn-out officers' uniforms, thin and with scorched faces. They surprised us at the entrance to the plant. Excited, I fell into his arms. His lips felt familiar; his scent was foreign.

We hurried home. Bruno looked at him with suspicion and refused to hug his estranged father. Maurizio went to visit his mother and returned shortly after to a table filled with delicacies I made for him. As I groomed myself for our lovemaking, he fell asleep still wearing his uniform and woke up twenty hours later.

When he opened his eyes, they were smiling at me, while his mouth told of a useless war and a continent of poverty and hunger. He told of screams of pain and the stench of death. My ears heard, but my heart refused to believe. For the first time since we married, the tension of alienation stood between us. Maurizio came back from the war withdrawn and pensive, whereas, during his absence, I turned into an independent woman.

It took us some time to get re-acquainted, to bond again. The war brought Maurizio and his younger brother together. The homecoming lit the fire of love under Lina and Emanuelle, and in our new routine, we went out, the four of us, quite a lot. Bruno was growing fast, and the relationship between him and his father grew as well.

But the aftershocks of the war that was, were the tell-tale signs of the war to come.

Every night, Maurizio would read me the words of the news commentators that kept promising that nothing bad would happen to any Jew in Italy. But Emanuelle, who spoke German and listened to Hitler's speeches on the radio, passionately claimed that Hitler was bad news, and therefore—despite Mussolini's declaration in 1935 that "There is no Jew problem in Italy," and despite the two brother's' participation in the war and their officers' ranks and money—grave danger lurked in our own home.

Tension crept into our pleasant daily routine. The idyllic relationship between Maurizio and Emanuelle gave way to constant differences of opinion they had about Hitler and what was happening in Germany at the time.

Tension, for very different reasons, seeped into the relationship of their father and his brother Jacob. Samuelle had taken responsibility for the extended family from a very young age and made his brother Jacob a junior partner in the business. Jacob's wife, Leticia, was a plain-looking woman and friendly. She and Josephina disliked each other. Samuelle, who was the older brother that provided for all of his siblings, was kind, and his wife, *Señora* Josephina, expected gratitude for it.

During the war in Ethiopia, when his sons were far away

from home, Samuelle made quite a few successful real estate deals. The family's fortune continued to grow, its business kept expanding, and my responsibilities grew as well. *Señor* Samuelle and I went together to check out the *Castello*, which was up in the mountains. It was a beautiful mansion that had vineyards, tennis courts, stables, a magnificent dining room and a banquette hall. Samuelle purchased it for a bargain price, and conceited Josephina was now also "The Lady of the Mansion."

That same year, on Josephina's birthday, Leticia bought her a present she did not like. "Keep your presents, and I'll keep mine, and we shall save the tip," Josephina hissed through tight lips. With teary eyes, Leticia commanded her sons to leave the party with her and never set foot in the big house again.

The next morning, Jacob and Samuelle closed themselves in the office for many hours. Even Maurizio, who sided with Leticia, wasn't allowed in. Around noon, the door opened, and the four boys and I were invited in. Samuelle informed us that they regretfully decided to part ways. I was asked to type up the necessary documents and stayed next to Mr. Samuelle for many hours after the brothers' handshake, trying to comfort him without words.

A month later, Jacob, together with his family, moved to Milan, where he opened a rival business under the name of "Vitale." Samuelle was furious and turned to the courts, which compelled Jacob to change the name or close the business. Jacob closed the business and emigrated with his family to America.

My husband and his brother muttered, *"Cherchez la femme"* ("Look for the wife" in French), whereas I made sure I pleased my mother-in-law with especially pricey gifts.

World War II started a short while after that. It was at the edge of our lives, "attacking" whoever wished to hear the news. Prices of gasoline escalated, unemployment increased, and rumors regarding the conduct of the Germans in Europe started to filter in, but the media never gave a clear picture of the situation. I learned on one of my visits to Vercelli that Mussolini's mistress Margarita had gone to Argentina.

I admit it didn't turn on any warning lights for me. All I cared about was that I managed to finish all my tasks on time, so I could spend time with Maurizio and hear his interpretation of the situation. He believed in Mussolini, and as an officer who fought in Ethiopia had faith in the Italians.

It was easy to believe him. He was tall with a mustache, funny and bitter alike, and he came back to love me. I loved the life he provided for me, I loved Bruno, rejoiced with Lina, and never let the news spoil my mood.

Ra E' Molto Pio Vicina
(A Distant War is Approaching)

"Wars within the family unit are many times a sign of wars outside," my mother, Anetta, said to me one morning in her kitchen. Vercelli was always "home" to me, and missing my parents caused me to catch the train from time to time to go visit them.

We planned to leave after breakfast for a morning walk with Bruno, who had grown up to be quite a captivating little boy. The terror I felt in the first few months of his life were now forgotten, and when he was five and a half years old, I found myself expecting again.

I realized it by the morning sickness I felt for the first time that morning, upon reading the news about the new race laws that came into effect that day that made the Jews in Italy citizens without rights.

At my parents' house, Judaism wasn't taken seriously. Life next to our Christian neighbors was conducted in harmony, and we only visited the synagogue on special occasions and high holidays. The Vitale clan didn't conduct themselves religiously either. Samuelle maintained that education was the most important thing and sent his four sons to study at the finest universities in Europe. It was clear to everyone that business could be done with everyone, but marriage was only possible with the daughters of Israel.

I saw the headline in the newspaper folded on my mother's table, and as she served me the *fagiolini* (a green bean dish) I really loved, I felt sick to my stomach for the first time. When I continued to read, I realized I would not be able to register Bruno at the public school the coming school year. Later, when I called Celeste worried, I learned that her sons were home schooled with a private teacher, and that tensions were high in Milan as well, despite her husband's vast connections.

The next day, I arrived at work white as a sheet. I suspected I was pregnant, but I didn't want to say anything until I was certain of it. I explained to worried Samuelle that I was concerned with the situation.

"I already spoke to Maurizio about it," my loving father-in-law hurried to reassure me. "We will organize a room here, find a teacher, and Bruno will study here with the rest of the children.

"But you are pale…" he added.

"I am fine," I said to him and got up to make us coffee. Lina had just given birth to sweet Anna. I hoped that soon I could make Maurizio and Samuelle happy with my news. I also hoped that I would have a daughter this time.

Emanuelle was the first to internalize what was happening around us. "We have to change the business name," he insisted, as the rest of the brothers refused to be rattled by the articles in the newspapers.

The debate became heated when Emanuelle quoted what

was written with regard to the Jews: "It is forbidden (a) to be members in the fascistic party; (b) to own or manage factories that employ a hundred or more employees; (c) to own more than fifty square meters of land; (d) to serve in the military in times of peace or in times of war. The activities of these Jews will be regulated by laws to be approved in the future." The race laws of fascistic Italy.

Samuelle came out of his office when he heard the shouting. "Come inside," he ordered his sons, and only I noticed how much he had aged. Within a few hours, the paperwork for changing the name of the business was ready. The veteran foreman of the plant, Joseppe, was called into the office and became the official owner of Samuelle Vitale's life's work.

With trembling hands, I took the signed papers from them. The light in Samuelle's eyes was gone.

Maurizio smiled at me attempting to cheer me up. "How are you feeling?" his lips whispered without uttering a sound.

"So, so," I replied, trying to figure out if he had guessed already. In the following three months, I tried to adjust to the morning sickness, and the Jews of Italy tried to adjust to the new situation.

Leggi Razziali
(Racial Laws)

During these months, Samuelle asked for my presence more and more. For many hours, he would have me sit at his side in his office, and with my help, he organized the finest details of the business.

"This is not hard for you, is it?" he would ask and sneak a peek at my bulging stomach. I felt he was almost as happy as Maurizio about the pregnancy, but at the same time, he looked old and sad.

Michelangelo's expulsion from the tennis club that he himself had established in Biella got us women worried. The insult, though, brought Michelangelo to the decision to renovate the *Castello* and the tennis courts in it. He allegedly went on with his life at the renovated *Castello*, played tennis, threw parties, but something about his behavior became more aggressive.

He grew a wild beard and, once in a while, he disappeared for a few days, and when he returned, always without notice, all he talked about was brigades and the organization of the resistance.

At home, almost all our conversations revolved around the

situation. My sister Lina was deeply affected by Emanuelle and didn't stop from warning us of the terrible danger lurking for us all. Compared to them, Maurizio and my father remained complacent, and Celeste felt safe in Milan with her husband, who was linked to the government.

I wanted to rely on Maurizio's peace of mind, but I began to dream about Napoleon again after a few years during in which I didn't. In my dreams, my little brother, who reminded me of Bruno a little, was running away from the Germans. I would wake up in a sweat, unable to go back to sleep. Maurizio, who would wake up, too, because of me, would sooth me by making love to me, dulling the fear.

At the beginning of April, right before Lina's birthday, Emanuelle came into the big house holding a large envelope. He placed it on the already set *Shabbat* table. "Open it," he said to Samuelle.

Inside the envelope, rested entry visas for America, fifteen of them. I will never forget the look of joy on Emanuelle's face when he counted the visas: Josephine, Samuelle, Alberto, his wife Elsa, Michelangelo, Maurizio, Vittoria, Bruno, Aunt Emilia, Aunt Ada (Samuelle's sister) and her husband 'and another three visas for whichever maid Josephina wanted to take with her.

For a moment, it was dead silent, and then the bomb blew up. Maurizio and Alberto were furious. "Is that what you spent one hundred thousand *lirettas* on, and risked sneaking across the border?!"

"You are all blind! You just don't understand what is going to happen here!" he answered in anger and looked lovingly at

Lina, who held Anna in her arms.

"It will be impossible to work, impossible to go on with our lives. Already, the kids are not allowed to go to school, and we're not allowed to run the business we built with our own two hands. We're not even allowed inside the bank anymore, and it's going to get worse. Hitler will not leave any Jew alive. He will annihilate the Gypsies, too, anyone who isn't blond with blue eyes will be destroyed."

Josephina tried to calm her sons down. The aunts were sobbing, Lina kept quiet, and I was thinking about my parents and my Aunt Celeste.

"Hitler will return all the Jews to the Ghettos. It is already happening in Rome. They are rotting in the ghetto and are not allowed to work in their professions. Jews in Germany are being sent to labor camps in Poland all the time. This is not going to end well. We can still run away. We can leave the business to Joseppe, and after the war, we can come back" Emanuelle tried to convince us again.

"You are mad," Maurizio roared and signaled me to pick up Bruno. We left the house. Maybe, if we had stayed a little longer and talked, everything would have been different. But Maurizio was not a man of words. He got up and left. This was the first time in my life, I went after him against my will.

I was left baffled. On the one hand, my father and my husband were promising me that everything would be all right, and on the other hand, maybe Emanuelle understood what the others refused to see. Lina came to us, crying, and announced that they were leaving in two weeks, emigrating to America. How would I live without her? How could she not be with me during the labor that was drawing near? We sat together in the kitchen crying bitterly.

Years later, every time we met, we would cry about the memory of that evening. In hindsight, I know that Maurizio was naïve. Unlike in business, here he didn't recognize the danger. As a retired officer and with many assets, he was positive that we were immune to any calamity, and even when he was asked to return his officer ranks, he did not understand that the ground was burning under us.

Nascita
(Giving Birth)

Two weeks after that day, Samuelle died in his sleep without warning. In his last couple of days alive, he mourned Emanuelle's departure and said repeatedly, "My children will be scattered around the world."

I tried to comfort and console him. "They will go and come back when the war is over." A month exactly after the ownership of the company transferred to the hands of the foreman, who we believed to be loyal, Samuelle closed his eyes forever, leaving me orphaned.

His four sons walked behind his shrouded body in silence. The whole town walked with him on his final journey, showing respect to the man who was, first and foremost, a human being.

I did not attend the funeral, as pregnant women were not allowed in the cemetery, but I attended the *Shiva*, and heard talk and debate all around me regarding the question, how well would the Germans succeed with their plans?

The word *Tedesco* was spoken in a whisper. "Germans" was a general synonym for everything undesirable. It was they who caused Emanuelle and Maurizio to fight, and it was because of them that Michelangelo grew a beard, had surrounded himself with people we did not know and wandered around on the roads. It was because of them that the sales went down, and many of our Italian acquaintances and neighbors couldn't look us in the eye.

At the *Shiva*, everyone talked about America as well. Lina and Emanuelle postponed their trip for a month, and at the end of the thirty days of mourning, Josephina announced that she was joining them.

Crying bitterly, without knowing for how long, we sisters parted with each other. On the day that Lina left, Ricardo started moving inside me, and I knew that in four and a half months, he would be born.

Samuelle's death left a void both in the business as well as my heart. I was forced to spend my time in the offices for hours, making sure that all was done according to his "word," as the business was no longer in our name.

I was pretty far along with Ricardo's pregnancy, and Bruno was attending the improvised Jewish preschool that was organized in the offices when Carlotta came to our home to work as a nanny for the baby that was yet to be born.

Hundreds of times I blessed my good fortune that eyes met her gray eyes as she stood at her sister's cheese stand in the Biella market I visited with six-year-old Bruno. The second time I was there, she hesitated a little at the sight of my smile and asked me in an Italian accent I wasn't familiar with if I would like her to come and do the cleaning at my house.

The old maid, Armenia, had abandoned us because she was uncomfortable working for Jews, and Carlotta, with her

Treviso Veneto[3] diction, came into our lives and helped prepare the house for the upcoming birth.

Carlotta's entry into our house was felt everywhere. Every corner became cleaner and brighter, and every fabric, more ironed. It seemed as if she managed to remove the dust before it made its way to the furniture, and the delicacies that she made in the kitchen gave me much pleasure during the pregnancy.

I distinctly remember the taste of the dark zucchini that melted in your mouth like French fries. I devoured bowls of this food, despite the heartburn that followed almost immediately.

Bruno, who was learning to read at the time, would ask, confused, if Carlota's *Santa Maria* was like the Jews' *Shma Israel*, and would receive detailed answers from Maurizio that every religion had its own God, and that all people were good. Well, almost everyone. Hitler wasn't. He was a *Tedesco*—a German.

On the day Ricardo was born, Maurizio took Bruno out with his bicycle and Carlota stayed with me, holding my

---

3   Treviso is a city in the province of Veneto in Northern Italy and serves as the capital of the Treviso district. Home to 82,854 residents as of the census of November 2010, the city is also known as the home of the fashion company Benetton, named after Luciano Benetton, and is also known for their basketball team Benetton Treviso, which is sponsored by the Benetton Company. The city is also known as the original production place of the Prosecco wine and the Tiramisu dessert.

hand. Ricardo came out into the arms of the midwife, and the whole birthing experience was soft and pleasant. I hoped in my heart that maybe this was a good omen.

But Samuelle's absence was felt in everything, especially during the circumcision party. Fewer people came this time to the ceremony, which was held at the synagogue, than when Bruno was born, and I never stopped crying.

Alberto's daughters were around me, looking at my incessant crying with wonder. It was my first time in the synagogue without Samuelle, and from my family, only my parents and my sister Celeste arrived.

It was weird to be at my son's circumcision ceremony without my father, without Lina, my sister, or Emanuelle and Anna, without Josephina. The war hovered over us all. All of a sudden, I felt like a guest in my own life. I could hardly listen to Maurizio, who conducted the ceremony. I knew he was about to announce my son's name—Ricardo—and all I wished for was that the pain from the milk overfilling my breasts would go away.

I vaguely remember the nights I hardly slept in the first few weeks after Ricardo's birth, and in the background—the confusing war.

We didn't know what was happening in Europe. It was slow to occur and far away. The hope that the war would not reach us caused us to hear what we wanted in Mussolini's speeches, and we didn't want to hear what was really happening in Europe. Although it was impossible not to see that business had slowed down, and the rules had changed, we were living our lives as if inside a bubble. We were very busy with baby

Ricardo, Bruno and with Alberto's daughters. The Italian workers kept coming to work, and even when the sales lessened, socks and uniforms were still being vigorously sewn. Since we were the employers of most of the town's residents, we felt immune.

Ricardo's birth was the first joyous occasion after Samuelle passed away. Bruno, who was used to being an only child until the age of six, was suddenly the older brother. All his cousins and the babies he met so far were guests for a minute, but baby Ricardo was there to stay, and before my child had a chance to get used to his little brother, I was started putting on weight again.

Carlota was the first one to notice. She gave me her direct look and said, "Mrs. Vitale, you are pale."

Before sweet Ricardo turned four months, I was pregnant again. "Children are joy," said Maurizio.

I prayed for a girl and hoped that Carlota would remain with us. The help at home became scarce with the rise of the fascists into power. People were afraid to work for Jews, but Carlota wasn't affected by it. In time, I learned of her story, and why, despite the fact she was a devoted Catholic, she chose to work specifically in the homes of Jews.

Fossalta Di Piave Italia
(Carlota's Birthplace)

Carlota, so she told me much later when we became very close, was born in the province of Treviso Veneto,[4] where they spoke a dialect called Veneto. Her hometown, *Fossalta Di Piave*, was a poor town near Venice.

She was born on Good Friday, 6 April 1905, which, according to the Catholic calendar, is the Friday before Easter. It was her mother's seventh childbirth, and the family already had four sons and two daughters. Carlota's parents made a living working in odd jobs, and her mother's frequent pregnancies made it impossible for her to hold onto any permanent position. At the home Carlota was born into, they believed strongly in the holy trinity, in the fact that Jesus walked on water, and in everything the priest told them at the Catholic Church.

None of the children in the family went to school, as they had no money. They were sent to work at a very young age. At home, there was very little food, but despite the poverty and the struggles to survive, the home was filled with love and joy.

---

4   Explained in previous footnote.

Her mother and father found comfort in the arms of one another and didn't even bother to conceal their fondling from the children. Of all of the children, only Carlota was repelled by this sight. She thought of these physical acts as fools' condemnation and believed, with all her heart that if she stayed celibate and observed Christianity, her luck would change. Deep inside, she hoped that the family would allow her to join a convent and become a nun, but as soon as she turned twelve, she was sent to work as a maid for a wealthy Venetian family.

Her job was to do all the cleaning of the entire huge house. It was a lavish house, filled with mirrors and wooden furniture that needed polishing—that is how Carlota described it to me—a big house, and in all three stories of it, lingered a scent of vanilla mixed with lilies, a dense and overwhelming smell.

On her first day, she was greeted by a rainstorm and a variety of cleaning jobs that waited for her in the stuffy house. She felt sick to her stomach. The household's personal butler, an older solemn man with thick eyebrows, kept moving past her again and again, staring at her with lustful eyes.

At seven o'clock in the evening, when she could finally retire to her room with the crucifix she brought from home, she sighed in relief. She shared a room with the two daughters' nanny, a grumpy condescending woman who never exchanged one word with Carlotta.

Every night, she prayed to Jesus, God and Maria, asking that the next day, her body would ache less from the hard work of moving from room to room in that enormous house trying to make it clean.

Sundays were the days she could visit church, pray and meet her family, and by evening, she would report back at the home of the rich family that never lifted a finger to do anything. She wanted nothing from them. She had her own order to things, and no one interfered with it. With every week that passed, the work became easier, and all that troubled her was to escape the butler with the bushy eyebrows who never ceased his attempts to grab her. He would wait for her on the stairwell, fondling a watch in his hands with his eyes blazing at her. She felt as if his looks were defiling her body, but looking was not enough for him. When she was busy working, he would come from behind, touching her and whispering lewd remarks at her.

She knew she must not let him defile her. Haunted, she ironed her clothes every night to cleanse herself from his looks and touch.

She had no protection from him, not even a soul to share her predicament with. But one Sunday, when she was old enough to decide her own fate, she heard from her parents that they were moving up north to look for work in the area of Biella, and she decided to leave the stifling house with the hated stalker and join them.

To her misfortune, the nightmare that began at the family's home in Venice, repeated itself with the family she worked for on the outskirts of Milan. This time, the father of the family came after her himself. She was young and strong, and when he tried to forcibly lay her down, she slapped him and ran away from that house.

She found a temporary safe haven at her parent's house, sleeping on an old sofa. She then made up her mind to never marry and to save her virginity for the sake of Jesus and redemption. She held onto her faith with all her might. She already knew all the prayers by heart, but her dream was to learn to read and write, so she could read the scriptures herself. Every week, she would go to church and listen with utmost attention to the sermons at mass, but all she heard there were blasphemers and accusations about the Jews. They blamed the Jews for all the evil in Italy and the entire world: poverty, misfortune and anything bad that happened.

Deep in her heart, so Carlota told me, she was doubtful it was true. Then, while she was sleeping on the couch at her parent's house and every morning going to help her sister at the cheese stand in the Biella market, she met Mrs. Vitale, who came there to buy cheese. What appealed to her in particular, so she said, was the look on the boy's face, a serious illusive look that appeared when she looked at him. Something in the boy's appearance told her he wasn't Christian. Her decision to offer her services and work for the Jews was her revenge for the last person who harassed her. To her joy, Mr. Vitale, the father of the family, looked at her in an untarnished manner, and it was clear to see that he, as a man, loved only his wife.

To my joy, Carlota integrated into our family as if the position were always waiting for her. She loved Bruno from the first moment she saw him at the Biella market and was thrilled when I suggested she sit with him when he was home schooled.

Carlota thanked Jesus for her good fortune, and although

the chatter all around was that it was dangerous to come in contact with the Jews, she felt that, in our home, she had found her calling. She had no problem with us being Jews, our customs, or our prayers. She worshiped Maurizio for abstaining from alcohol and for the way he treated his wife.

She was very perceptive and hard-working, and understood everything I taught her immediately. Instead of listening to the hateful message the priest would deliver in church about the Jews, as she told me, she was now able to read the scriptures herself. Her greatest pleasure was to learn together with Bruno reading, arithmetic, and science. A new world had opened up to her, and she blessed her cleaning jobs, as when she did the laundry and ironing she could memorize the new things she learned. When Aldo was born, she was already a full member of the family, and she loved him and bonded with him.

I gave birth to Aldo two weeks prematurely, on a fairly hot day of the 27th of July, 1940. In hindsight, I realize it was in the midst of the war.

Aldo was born to the disappointment he wasn't a girl but was very quick to find his place. His lively smile, flexible body movements, keen sense of survival and the charm of being the third to be born created a situation where very quickly he caught up with Ricardo, and they walked around like twins. In a year and a half, we turned from a couple with a six-year-old to a family with three children.

To my good fortune, Carlota was there with us. There was something in her clear, pleasant look that I loved. She was there with Bruno, with whom she sat and studied the lessons

I taught, with Ricardo and Aldo, who grew up in her lap, and with us, Maurizio and I, who kept working and taking care of the business, or at least we tried to.

Lina and Samuelle were sorely missed. Maurizio talked a great deal about Emanuelle, and even wrote him letters. Josephina's absence was deeply felt, and Alberto visited the office a lot.

In the summer of 1943, on the last ship arriving from America, *Señora* Josephina returned to Italy.

To my questions about my sister Lina and my brother-in-law, she replied that Emanuelle was busy in his own business manufacturing men's clothes, and Lina was with the kids. She also said that in America, everyone had no manners, and they were less polite. Lina and Emanuelle's children spoke English, she said with discontent, and she was not sure they would know Italian. It was true that between them, Emanuelle and Lina conversed in Italian, but the rest of the time, they spoke English.

Josephina said the word "America" with reservation, and that was how she spoke of the coffee and pasta they served over there. I wasn't surprised to hear her criticism of America, not even of my sister and my brother-in-law that became too "American" in her opinion, but she managed to surprise me with something else.

When *Nonna* ("Grandmother") Josephina entered our home after the long journey, she met Carlota, who was with Aldo and Ricardo in the dining room. Carlota, who heard about her from us, introduced her new grandchildren to her, and *Señora* Josephina smiled at her with weary eyes. Until that moment, I had never seen *Nonna* Josephina smile at a maid or a nanny; she also only hugged her grandchildren in extreme situations.

After that encounter, which was surprisingly warm, Carlota won Josephina's heart with her tomato *gnocchi*, and veal and potato roast she prepared for the first dinner *Señora* Josephina had at our house after returning from America.

The war had stripped Italy of its resources, and for us as Jews, and as a couple with three children, it was difficult to provide all the necessities, but Carlota managed to run the household in such a way that the aroma of her dishes and delicacies welcomed us at every meal.

La Guerra
(The War)

At the end of 1942, my father passed away in his sleep from cardiac arrest. His funeral was small and sad, and a complete contrast to his life, which was full and joyous. Only a handful of relatives from Vercelli gathered, and my mother insisted on foregoing the *Shiva*. Without Lina and the two babies I had to take care of, it was redundant. Jews didn't venture out of their homes much, and sure enough didn't gather. So, his death, unlike his life, went by quietly. I regretted that Aldo and Ricardo didn't get to meet my father's self-indulgent temper.

Even if we didn't want to hear or see it, the war was raging in Europe, and there were many signs that it would reach us in Italy as well. Once in a while, we would hear a plane crossing the sky. Maurizio's Aunt Ada, who lived in Rome, vanished and no one knew how to find her, and the contact with family that lived far away from us became scarce. The factory was still manufacturing uniforms for the army, but there was much less work, and the fuel was running out. The Vitale brothers would whisper a lot between them about the chances that Germany would be defeated by the Allied

Forces. Fewer and fewer people smiled at us on the street, fewer people roamed the streets at night, our children studied at the office with a teacher that didn't always show up, contact with mother and Big Celeste wasn't as often, letters from Lina barely arrived, and conversations with my sister Celeste were spoken in a different tone.

In this reality—this new reality—Carlota was with me, and my soul bonded with hers. It was her I told how I missed Lina and Samuelle, and it was before her that I laid my deepest concerns about the future that awaited us.

The influence of the war brought with it more changes. Michelangelo, whose father's death made him more serious, became very close to us. This young brother, Michelangelo, who to me always seemed like a child, matured a lot during the war. His reddish beard grew and became a part of his beautiful face, and he wore his red hair back. Each time he came for a visit, I could feel his gaze measuring my body. He would sit in the kitchen, lift the children one by one in the air, and make us all laugh. He spent hours in my kitchen, after which he would take all the cash out of the cash register, pack up all the leftovers and go up to the *Castello*. This *Castello* that Samuelle bought before he died became somewhat of a headquarters to him. I loved his presence. In the face of his lusting looks, I felt like a pretty woman.

Secretly, he told me of the weapons he bought and smuggled out with that money. He also told me what was happening to the Jews in Eastern Europe, in Poland especially. He told me of the concentration camps where Jews were being thrown into pits. I didn't want to believe.

And so, with all the horror stories he would tell and the war that kept on raging in Europe, Michelangelo suggested he would take the kids and *Nonna* Josephina to the family beach house in the town of Bordighera, in which there were a few artifacts he could trade with, and Maurizio and I could have a nice rest. I did not know at the time that for Michelangelo, who was entirely preoccupied with the Italian resistance, actively trading and fighting against the Germans, this trip to Bordighera was a cover up to smuggle God knows what.

The news wasn't reported as frequently as it is nowadays. We would listen to the news on the radio, which sometimes worked and sometimes didn't. On the radio, they did not report what the Germans did in the war, but only what was happening in Italy. They spoke of the government, the economic situation, and the German invasion of Italy, after conquering Poland, Russia, and Austria—which brought on a certain commentary about the takeover—but it remained unclear as to what was really happening in the war, or at least in Italy. It felt as if the war was about to end soon. We heard rumors about the atrocities that took place in the work camps, but news about what was really happening did not reach us. We were complacent, so much so, that when we were alone that night, Maurizio and I went to bed and made love like we used to. That night, I thought a little less about Michelangelo, and Maurizio looked beautiful and full of plans to me. There was something in the way he held me and made love to me that gave me the feeling that everything was going to be all right.

"Don't worry," I managed to hear before I dozed off in his loving embrace like before. "We will get through this. I think that Michelangelo found a way to communicate with Ada and the family."

I woke up into darkness, hearing the metal click of the door latch and Maurizio's panicked mumbling. The time was six o'clock in the morning. A minute later, he stood above me, "The Germans are here. They are warning us. It is happening much faster than I anticipated. We need to bring them back."

It was the neighbor lady who sent her son to warn us. It was all part of the being a in an important family in town, the fact that everyone knew we were Jews. Our neighbors, with a great risk to themselves, warned us despite their fear of the Germans.

I jumped out of bed, got dressed and ran to the phone, which was recently installed in our home. It was disconnected. I took out the suitcase and started packing.

"Let's go call from the office," Maurizio told me. The sun wasn't up yet, and we both ran in our coats carrying what little silver we had in our house to the office. All my feelings of security and pleasantness faded away. It was freezing cold, and the fear in Maurizio's eyes reflected the fear in mine. We hid the silverware in the safe and tried to establish contact with Bordighera.

"Hello," answered *Nonna* Josephina in a sleepy voice.

"Please come back," Maurizio told her. "Where is Michelangelo?"

"He should be back in a little while. He went out last night and said he would return today. I'll ask Carlota to get organized. "*Che Cce*?" (What happened?)

"Come back, and we will talk in Biella," said Maurizio.

The employees coming to work in the factory could be seen in the courtyard. "Go through the side streets," Maurizio told me. "I'll stay here."

He took out all the cash from the safe and placed it in my hand. "TO, you already know what to do with this money." I remembered there was more money in there, but I didn't utter a word. I understood that the man we entrusted the business to was taking money for himself. We had nothing to say anyway. We were in his hands.

When I came home, the neighbors' shutters were closed, and the wind was blowing. At home, Alberto was waiting for me. The news about the Germans arrival reached him as well. I sent him to the factory, and it was agreed that he would return with Maurizio. I prayed to God to keep my children safe and to watch over Michelangelo, too.

Suddenly, I felt in a war, and my children were not near me. I heard it around me all the time, but now it was here, in the city, on the street, in my courtyard. It was clear that we needed to get organized and escape. I debated what to pack first and started sewing, with very unprofessional hands, inner pockets in our coats. Every once in a while, I laid down the sewing and went through the rooms like a storm, not knowing what to take care of first. The feeling of helplessness was infused with a crazy energy and the need to take over the packing so as not to lose control of the situation.

We waited for a few hours in the closed-off house, afraid to open the shutters. Outside, the sound of the German motorcycles and the clicks of their boots could be heard. The sound of a door slamming reminds me of that fear to this day.

Around noon, Alberto went to his house, bundled his wife and daughters, and took them to the *Castello*. At nightfall, carrying a little food and two suitcases for the days ahead, Maurizio and I walked over there. We knew that Michelangelo would not come to our home but there. It was obvious he was smuggling stuff and would unpack it there first.

We paced between the rooms at the *Castello* biting our nails in anxiety, waiting for Josephina, the kids and Michelangelo to arrive. I trusted Michelangelo to bring them home safely, but couldn't stop worrying. Shortly before sunrise, I heard the tires of the car squeaking on the gravel path. I was sitting in the kitchen, busy sewing inner pockets in the boys' and Maurizio's coats. The children looked pale and panicked. I held them in silence. Not knowing what the right thing to say was. Was it over? Was it beginning?

Bruno told me in excitement how they hid in the truck. I felt a cold shiver running down my spine. How did I let them travel like that on roads packed with the German army trucks?

I cried. Bruno looked at me baffled, and I just hugged him without saying a word. I remember that hug; I remember the innocence in his eyes. If I could stop time at that point in the kitchen, I would. But time did not stop, and life would never be the same again.

We were naïve to think we could get far from the city, to hide with our Christian acquaintances in the mountains. We pushed out any thoughts of escaping Italy. We believed with all our might that in a few weeks, it would all end and life would get back on track.

The faithful and loyal Carlota, who had been with us for five years by then, suggested we run away to her home village. "The children will be with me, and you can stay with a friend of mine."

Maurizio surprised me and nodded in acceptance. For the past twenty-four hours, since the Germans entered Biella, he had thought we would hide in the mountains, but once Carlota suggested we go with her to her village, he neglected his escape plans and just followed her. We decided to run to Treviso, Carlota's birthplace.

Inverno
(Winter)

While we waited in the *Castello* for the night to be over so we could leave, I couldn't stop crying, trying to suppress the vague feeling we might never return there. Maurizio hovered around me, gray and worried, lighting one cigarette after another with a helpless, angry look on his face. The two younger boys fell asleep, exhausted from the road, and only Bruno paced around restless, trying to understand what the morning would bring.

We didn't explain anything to the kids. We were unable to, as we ourselves did not understand what was going on. The Germans took over Biella. The Jewish businesses closed, and so did our factory, which hadn't been in our name for a while. The few Jews in town fled like frightened mice. It wasn't clear what happened to those who were captured. The Germans looked for Jews and Gypsies. Although the Italians did not cooperate with their conquerors, they did not resist either. They only tried to live their lives in peace.

It was a cold winter's morning when we left, riding our bikes like we were on our way to a picnic in the mountains. The fear caused even our younger children to keep completely silent.

The time to say good-bye came at noon. Maurizio decided to stay at a friend's house not far from town, and the kids continued on their way to the village with Carlota. I couldn't control the shiver that took over my body. It was only Carlota's presence that kept me from bursting into tears. The anger that welled up inside me for letting ourselves be complaisant, for not escaping in time with Emanuelle and Lina, was infused with the sorrow of parting with the children. I held them, refusing to let go until Maurizio ripped them from my arms and urged Carlota to hurry and continue on their way.

Trembling, I looked at Maurizio with hate. He looked at me surprised. I had never treated him like that before. Suddenly, it became clear to me that he, too, just like the kids, could not be without me. He needed me to prepare food for him, and I was his comfort in the bedroom and his life partner and friend. At that moment, I realized to my horror that parting with the children was meant to keep him safe, too. The children loved Carlota and loved the adventure. I hated. I hated the war, hated the separation from my children, and hated Maurizio.

In the first few days, early in the morning, I would get on my bike and ride up the mountain to meet the children. Maurizio rode to the *Castello* and joined Michelangelo and his friends that ran the resistance against the Germans, and at nightfall, we would meet. Every night, I told Maurizio about the day's events. He was concerned that Bruno 'wasn't learning and not reading enough. To this day, I am amazed by the fact that this was what occupied his thoughts at the time.

Winter crawled down the mountain, and I found myself

trying to make my way in the snow. The kids spent more and more time closed off in the barn by themselves, with Carlota feeding them and trying to make their stay pleasant. Apart from Michelangelo, who came every now and again, the contact between the extended family and us was severed.

Winter was in full force, and the stories that came from different sources about what was happening in the whole of Europe and in Italy joined into a picture that left no room for doubt. Maurizio's cousin, Ada, was captured and sent to Auschwitz with her daughter. "Auschwitz" was a synonym word that meant "The End." Her sister went into hiding in Milan, and Alberto had already left the *Castello* with his wife for Switzerland, and on the way placed his two daughters in an orphanage in Italy.

Nora and Silvia, the two sweet girls that grew up with my boys, for whom I would buy pink dresses, were placed in an orphanage. Appalled, I asked Maurizio how Josephina had allowed that to happen.

Maurizio answered that the orphanages and boarding schools were the safest places to be during the war because there they were protected.

Years later, Nora told me how they shared two bottles of hot water that they passed from bed to bed in the freezing cold, with forty babies and toddlers. Her two-year-old sister, Silvia's body was covered in sores, and she, the older sister of four, watched over her. She couldn't remember the parting from her parents. She wasn't angry with them either. Alberto and his wife didn't know if they would be able to get over the border alive, and all they wanted was to protect the girls.

The winter was in full force. The days grew shorter, and riding the bike up the mountain became impossible. We were the last remaining survivors of the family in Italy, hiding with the help of Carlota. Alberto was already settled in Switzerland, and *Nonna* Josephina had also escaped to Switzerland. Carlota and her sister never complained, but it became obvious to all of us that we would have to flee Italy. I tried to figure out Maurizio's plan. I expected that, as a resourceful man as he always portrayed himself to be, he would have a plan. But to my disappointment, he did not have one.

Michelangelo, who by then was entirely a resistance man, had a plan for us. He described it to Maurizio and me. He told us that there was a school in Como, which was a meeting point for his friends in the resistance. There, they were passing people through the border on foot to Switzerland. *Nona* Josephina and Alberto were already there, together with more people we knew. It would be safe for us. It was just a night's walk. He already paid to whom it was required.

"The sooner we do this, the better," Michelangelo also said. The resistance was informed that the Germans were to meet in two days in Milan and would not be in Biella, which made it a good time to first go to the house and from there to Como. The plan was immediate.

Fuga Da Casa
(Running Away from Home)

Two months after leaving home in a panic, we came back one night and snuck into it. Looters had ruined everything; the house was messed up, and the silverware I kept from my wedding was gone. I packed what little was left. I didn't know that later on, whatever I packed would not arrive with us. It was clear the passage from Italy to Switzerland during December would not be easy. Maurizio suggested that we arrive in Como separately; I would go with Carlota, Michelangelo and the little ones, and he and Bruno would join us the next day. That night at our house, I realized it was possible we would never return to it again.

A few days earlier, Bruno had asked me when the war would be over, and did I think he would have to be a soldier like Michelangelo. Aldo and Ricardo stopped playing with the ball to hear my reply. I answered in a stifled voice that I 'didn't know, but they mustn't worry, as we were in good hands. We had connections, and 'it was going to be all right. I was trying to convince myself as well. I placed a lot of trust in Michelangelo, and many thoughts about him and the resistance filled my heart.

It was dark the morning we left on our journey. I remember the silhouette of the house in the dark, the neighbor's door opened a crack, the feeling that the Germans were lurking in every corner, and the sense of strangeness I felt in my own home and in the town where my boys were born.

Carlota, who was whole-heartedly a willing recruit for the mission, waited for us with a basket of provisions to take with us, all dressed up to go on the trip. A moment before she left, she washed the last of the dishes and left Bruno and Maurizio lunch and dinner all prepared in the fridge.

Maurizio held me tight, my body melting into his arms and my face washed with tears. He scolded me not to cry, but I couldn't stop the tears from falling. Bruno looked happy and panicked all at the same time. On the one hand, he was happy to go on a trip with his dad; on the other, he wasn't used to seeing me so weak.

So, with my face covered in tears, I left Bruno with Maurizio, and together with the two younger children and Carlota, we crammed into Michelangelo's friend's car, which waited outside to drive us to the train station. I knew we needed to get to the big high school near Como. First take the train to Milan and from there to Como.

Carlota, more focused than ever, was touching the crucifix on her neck. I sat in the car with my bra filled with money that Maurizio and I had shared the evening before, and with the little jewelry I had. Our passports were pinned to my stomach. Ricardo and Aldo did not understand what was happening and sat between us quiet and scared. We drove silently like this to the train station in Biella. The train station was filled with a mass of terrified refugees and German soldiers. At that moment, the war became real. I held the boys closer, while Michelangelo and Carlota whispered between them. With one boy at the age of two and a half and one at the age of three and a half, I could have never been saved if it weren't for her. I felt grateful she was with me. She risked herself for us. Indeed, she could have stayed in her home, knitting, foregoing the attempt to come with us.

The train arrived after a hellish half an hour. We boarded the train, crowding together with many people carrying their luggage. Michelangelo's tough appearance did not mislead me; he was terrified, too.

The locomotive's horn made me jump. The thought of Bruno staying behind made me burst into tears again into Ricardo's neck as he sat on my lap. Carlota hugged Aldo tightly, trying to spare him from my despair, looking angrily at me.

The trip to Milan, which was supposed to be over within an hour, took more than two and a half hours, with the train stopping at every possible station and herds of people boarding it.

In the grayish train station of Milan, I hurried with Michelangelo to look for the ticket office. After we had purchased tickets for Como, we settled at the proper dock. There were fewer people there than on the other docks, and I tried to create the look of travelers during the hour and a half we had to wait for our train to arrive. The boys played under Carlota's watchful eye, ignoring the train whistles and the shouts of the soldiers. Michelangelo tried to reach a pay phone to call Maurizio, but the line was too long so he had to give up that idea. The waiting prolonged and lasted three and a half hours. The train was two hours late. We arrived in Como in the evening. It was pouring rain, and in the darkness, we could see the shadow of a truck waiting for us. The driver let us off the truck next to the structure of an abandoned school. The main hall of the school was bustling with persecuted Jews. Ricardo and Aldo ate the last of the sandwiches in Carlota's basket and immediately fell asleep on the cold floor wrapped in my coat.

Profughi Ebrei
(Jewish Refugees)

It was cold, and the scent of urine and fear hung in the air. Dirty and desperate, I lay down next to the children, asking that slumber bestow a few hours of oblivion on me. But the fear and the worrying for Bruno left me awake almost until dawn.

That night—the first without Bruno—was when a big hole opened in my stomach, when worry started eating at me. There, in the gap that opened inside me, was where the tumor later settled and started gnawing my insides. I don't remember how I managed to fall asleep, but I recall waking up to the smell of urine in the hall and to the sound of persistent rain on the hall's roof.

I woke up on the cold floor of the gymnasium with worry spreading throughout my being that Bruno and Maurizio hadn't arrived yet. The story about what happened to Bruno, who stayed with Maurizio in the house after we left, I heard much later, from Bruno.

He said it was strange for him to be in the abandoned house without Carlota and without us. Maurizio went in and out of the house numerous times until that night, he arrived and ate his dinner in deafening silence, after which he said to Bruno, "Tomorrow morning we leave."

Ten-year-old Bruno was scared to disappoint his father, and that's why he had trouble falling asleep. He tossed and turned all night. When his father came to wake him, he was already sitting on the bed all dressed up holding the little bag that had been prepared for him the night before.

It was six o'clock in the morning when they arrived at the train station.

At the station, someone from town, who worked at the cheese shop on the street near our home, approached Maurizio and asked him, "Aren't you afraid the Nazis will take you?"

Maurizio didn't reply but pulled Bruno by the hand to his side. In the meantime, the train arrived, and Maurizio bent over to Bruno and said, "This man might tell on me. If so, I'd rather that you go to where TO is so they won't take you with me. They are taking people to labor camps."

The children called me "mother and Maurizio called me "TO," and when Bruno told me this story, the word "TO" sounded so peculiar in his mouth. Maurizio also told him, "In your pocket, there is a note saying where you need to go. If anyone asks you, tell them that your mother is there and that your father isn't with you. Here's the ticket. I will take the next train. When the train reaches Milan, you will meet me, and we will both board the train to Como, but we will not talk to each other.

"If anyone asks you who I am, act as if we don't know each other.

"We don't know each other," he said, and pushed Bruno into the train that had just stopped, as its door opened.

This was the scene that brought an end to my eldest boy's childhood. In retrospect, it seems to me that it was there that Maurizio decided Bruno was mature enough to go through the war by himself if only so he could be saved.

From what Maurizio added about the story, it was portrayed to me like this: Bruno entered the train and sat in the cart closest to the door. There, he saw a drunken man with no shoes, despite the winter of December 1943. He was afraid to sit next to him; therefore, he kept going to the seat behind the man and settled next to two nuns that kept mumbling prayers in Italian, with his ticket ready in his hand. When the conductor came around and asked him why he was traveling alone, he told him what Maurizio told him to say. "My mother is waiting for me in Milan."

This was the first time he lied. He was scared and sweaty and regretted the fact that he did not bring anything to eat. He didn't even have water on him, and the nuns gave him some murky tea during the trip.

I remember that moment I realized he had traveled alone on the train when he was only ten. If I only knew that was how things were going to turn out, I would have insisted he come with me. Maurizio never really discussed this with me. As far as he was concerned, Bruno was his older first born, and since he was, Maurizio just put him on the train to travel alone. For years, I wondered if he did the right thing. Maurizio was a strong and determined man, unfamiliar with the weaknesses of the world. We expected our children—just because they were "ours" and "made" of our own flesh and blood—to be like us in their thinking, character, and strengths.

This is the first time with all the medication I am taking, that I can really understand and feel what happened to Bruno, my child. For years, I went back and imagined those moments to myself. My boy, ten years old, sitting alone on the train, frightened to his core.

The train ride took forever, and with every stop, Bruno panicked all over again. He didn't know if he would see his father again, and mostly he was afraid the cheese shop vendor would inform the Germans about his father and Bruno would arrive at Como only to greet me with the horrible news that his father was taken.

When he talked to me about the trip, it was after he had arrived, but since I also took that road, I am sure he was terrified. I also know my son, and every time I think of his first train trip without me, I cringe.

Bruno told me that, at the train station in Milan, he turned to one of the nuns and asked her where the platform to Como was. The nuns escorted him silently to the dock, where he quietly waited for three hours for the train to arrive, seeing his father from afar. At some point, when no one was looking, Maurizio placed a sandwich and a canteen of water next to Bruno. The docks were packed with refugees from all over Italy, Bruno said. He saw poor children and bleary-eyed mothers, and he sighed in relief knowing his father was nearby. The road from Milan to Como was easier since he knew his father was on the train and that we would all reunite in Como. He made an effort not to think of any other possibilities, but the sight of the many soldiers that occupied every space of the train created a sense of anxiety that wouldn't leave him for days to come.

Michelangelo waited for them at the train station. Bruno smiled at the sight of his red-haired uncle and knew that everything was going to be all right. There was something in Michelangelo's height and smile that always managed to reassure Bruno. Because of the many soldiers on the platform, he didn't dare hug his uncle, but just walked next to him. Maurizio arrived as well, and together with twenty more people, they got into a truck that was meant to take them to the meeting place at the school in Como. Bruno knew some of the people with him as Jews from his hometown and the nearby towns. When they arrived at the abandoned school, I could see from a distance that he was pale and with a different look in his eyes. I remember his embrace—tight and clingy. He was happy to see us. Maurizio whispered in my ear the story about the man from the cheese shop but did not elaborate about Bruno's journey by himself. Although he told me later about the train ride, it was just the beginning...

Decisione Critica
(A Critical Decision)

The hall, where a large crowd of refugees assembled, was noisy and bustling. Hundreds of people, with parcels thrown on the floor in every corner, a mixture of words, shouting and sobbing. A multitude of human beings that all they had in common was the fact they were Jews, and the realization they had to escape. The lighting was minimal, the stench from the bathroom and the fact that we were surrounded by strangers created an atmosphere of unrest. Each family marked a territory for itself. Ricardo and Aldo were running around with a gaiety reserved only for children, and I collapsed on the dirty floor and followed Bruno and Maurizio circling the hall with my eyes, as they were trying to figure out who to turn to.

Suddenly, everything became quiet when a man wearing a tall hat entered the hall, and only the sound of hushing parents silencing their children remained in midair. I do not remember what he looked like, but I can't forget the pile of well-organized papers he was carrying. Those were documents and lists that had the power to affect each of our fates.

The men all hurried to gather around him, and once again, mayhem broke. I couldn't hear what was said, but from their disappointed faces when they each returned to their families, I understood the general idea. Maurizio and Michelangelo stayed next to him and kept on talking to him. I also saw an envelope of cash exchanging hands, but Maurizio's face looked grim when he returned to where I was sitting surrounded by many packages. I rose to him, with my whole body tensing. "It's impossible to pass through more than four people. Nothing helps, not money and not reasoning," he whispered in my ear attempting to prevent the children from panicking.

I looked around at the families that filled the hall. Children, elderly people, couples, my family among them, I was trying to divide the crowd into many quarters. I counted those belonging to me: Bruno, Carlota, Michelangelo, Aldo, Ricardo, Maurizio and I. Michelangelo declared last night that he will not run away, he'd rather stay in Italy by himself, hoping to keep an eye on the business. Maybe even join the Partisans. We were, therefore, six. "We cannot pass through more than four people." The blood ran out of my face, my knees were shaking.

Maurizio leaned over to Carlota and whispered something in her ear. She nodded her head, pulled out her passport from the bag and handed it to him.

Wondering, I followed the movements of his hand as he pulled out a pen from his coat's inner pocket and with a confident move wrote the word "Jew" in her passport. Without batting an eye, Carlota took off the golden crucifix from her neck and gave it to Michelangelo, who gave her an assuring smile.

Maurizio turned to me in a whisper, "We will pass with the little ones, and Bruno will come with Carlota." Bruno hadn't recovered from the trip, and the scare from the informant and the thought of leaving him again with Carlota and her fake passport terrified me. I couldn't stop my tears. Maurizio looked at me in anger. I collapsed into the pile of bags, sobbing. Aldo and Ricardo hurried to hug me. Bruno sat next to me, avoiding contact, with his eyes pinned to the ground. Carlota, Maurizio, and Michelangelo went to speak with the man in the hat, to try and convince him that at least we can go through on the same truck. I looked at my three children through a screen of tears, the cold paralyzed me, and the fear did not allow me to think clearly.

All I had left was to count on Maurizio's judgment, who ruled, "We will go through with the little ones. Carlota will take Bruno with her. They will get there." Bruno looked at me in question. I couldn't bring myself to provide him with any explanations. I pulled his clothes from the pile of bags and packed them separately in silence.

I then pulled out the sewing kit and a few gold coins. Blinded by tears, I unpicked the lining of his coat and sewed the coins into it. He just looked at me vaguely and silently. I leaned in to hug him, and I prayed. I prayed the whole time. I asked to be awakened from that nightmare. I asked for the war to be over, and for Hitler to be killed so we could go home. I wanted to die. I promised God that I would listen to Maurizio and that when the war was over, we would go to Israel. I promised that we would be in Jerusalem for the Day of Atonement, but each time I lifted my eyes, all of my prayers and vows faded into the smell of urine and fear that was everywhere.

Maurizio sat down next to us, took hold of Bruno's chin forcing him to look him in the eye. "It is impossible to get more than four through. I tried to give more money; I tried to persuade the guy. It is a full night's walk in the mountains; we will have to split up. You will pass through with Carlota. We will meet once you go through. We leave at dawn."

Maurizio's face was gray, his mustache trembled, but his eyes remained dry, and his voice determined. Bruno looked at him silently, nodding with acceptance. Maurizio kissed his forehead and turned to me. "Enough crying" he whispered at me in a commanding voice, but I, who never parted with Bruno for more than a couple of days, couldn't help myself.

Michelangelo bid us farewell. He kissed my kids on their heads, kissed me on both cheeks, gave his brother a strong hug and left the hall. At that moment, I envied him for not having children. Despite the fear and the unknown, despite the horror stories, I felt safe as long as he was near me. I was overwhelmed with a sense of helplessness. Maurizio's gray face told me he felt the same. Maurizio, who had always set the rules, had to face his weakness, his inability to control the situation. The damned war changed the rules of the game.

Slowly, the dark hall became silent. I lay down next to Bruno, who turned his back to me. I whispered stories in his ear and sang to him, all the lullabies I had used to put him to sleep with since he was born. I promised him again and again that we would soon meet beyond the border. Bruno wept softly, I cried without a sound, and none of us got any sleep that night.

At 3 a.m., we heard the truck arriving. I kissed Carlota, and kissed Bruno, refusing to break away from him. Maurizio tore Bruno from my arms and hastened me to get on the truck. He then approached the driver putting coins in his hand as he pointed at our bags. The driver, who was tired and smoked, grunted. We never saw our bags again.

Confine Di Montagna
(A Border in the Mountains)

The truck went on its way under cover of darkness. I sat on the floor of the truck with sleepy Aldo and Ricardo in my lap. My eyes continued to tear up. Maurizio sat next to me, tenderly stroking my shoulder. I leaned my head on his shoulder and woke up when the truck stopped. The cold was bone-chilling. A pale sun lit up the interior of the truck, and a thick smell of urine filled the air.

The driver rolled up the tarp cover at the back of the truck and rushed us to get off. Our luggage wasn't there, only the clothes on our backs, when all around us all one could see were snowy mountains.

The cigarette-smoking driver led us to a fence and told us to march alongside it until we saw an opening. First light broke in, and a thick fog covered the mountain. People started to fade into the mist, and the sun seemed to stop from rising to allow us to pass through the border into Switzerland.

Maurizio picked up Ricardo, and I took Aldo. A frozen humidity penetrated our bones. We walked heavily, hearing the squeaks of our shoes on the leaves and the frozen ice, searching the fence.

Without our luggage that disappeared with the truck, we were left without food or drinks. We marched into the unknown in a cloud of mist. In the moments when my stomachache threatened to get the best of me, I yearned to arrive in heaven through the same cloud. We walked for about a couple of hours. Most of the time, we carried our exhausted children on our shoulders until we reached the opening in the fence.

Maurizio lifted the children through the opening, and we went through. It was simpler than what I imagined. Switzerland. We didn't know where to go. Our aim was to be captured by soldiers and placed in a refugee camp. The concern that Carlota would not find the opening in the fence did not leave me. We kept going through the scenery that remained unchanged. Our bodies were screaming from fatigue, and the kids were crying from hunger. Dogs barking from afar caused me to quiver. Maurizio tried to reassure me and promised that the barking indicated there were Swiss soldiers nearby. Today, I know that we were very fortunate compared to what others had to go through in those days, but the horror of the march and the feeling of helplessness remained etched in my mind.

Here we were, marching with two small children. What would we give them to eat? Would we be able to reach safety? What was happening with my elder son, Bruno? All these questions were pecking at and sawing me from the inside as we walked like that on the ice in a mist. Now, with the tumor consuming me, I know it sprouted in the same pit that opened in my stomach during that march.

The fog started to lift, and in the clearing light, we could see a paved road.

We walked toward it, and when we heard a vehicle approaching, Maurizio ran in its direction and managed to stop a police jeep.

The cries of joy from the children when we were picked up by the police car reminded me of the ending scene in a Benigni film. There was so much optimism at that moment. I hurried to climb after them into the car mumbling the *Shma Israel* prayer, and praying that Bruno, too, would soon be picked up by them as well.

Svizzera Neutrale
(Neutral Switzerland)

The police officers brought us to the city's police station. A Swiss policewoman managed our registration as refugees with a cold indifference, and only after we begged her, was she willing to give a glass of water to my starving children. After the registration, we were loaded on a truck and driven to the gates of the refugee camp.

We waited outside the camp gates for three hours. The times of letting refugees in were organized, and there was protocol. As a refugee, you could not decide when someone would pay attention to you. I tried to calculate the travel time, trying to speculate when Bruno and Carlota will arrive.

Eventually, starved and exhausted, we were called into the admission office. Three serious-looking clerks welcomed us. Again, our certificates were presented, and our detailed information given. I made sure to give them any possible detail about Bruno and Carlota, but my questions regarding their prospects of arriving soon to camp remained unanswered.

At the end of the grueling process, we were led by a policewoman, who seemed indifferent, as if she was already accustomed to seeing refugee families, to a room with three bunk beds. The room was surprisingly clean and simple. The Swiss flag was displayed on the wall, and opposite the flag hung a faded scenery picture.

White sheets, a brown blanket, and even a little pillow were placed on each bed. The sight of six beds immediately breathed hope into me, that we will actually be reunited soon.

The scent of mold stood in the air, and the windows were divided into six squares and covered in dust. A structure, from which the smell of something cooking came, could be seen from the windows, and all of my stomach juices came to life. Next to it, was the bathroom building. The policewoman standing at the entrance explained the regulations to us, then pointed at the bathroom building and said that the children could shower with me only when there weren't any other women around. As for meals, she said that they informed through the speakers when to come to eat and that, from time to time, the refugees were also required to do chores. In the next few days, lists would be made, and if indeed, our relatives had arrived, they would be reunited with us. The last few words were said as she was already out in the hall. The narrow iron bunks squeaked as we lay on them exhausted, attempting to warm our frozen bodies with the military-issued woolen blankets.

The hunger did not leave us and overpowered the fatigue. As soon as the call was heard from the speakers, we hurried into the dining hall. The porridge that was served was tasteless but hot, and we ate it eagerly. The smell of cinnamon and warmed up Styrofoam is what I remember from it. Many details regarding our first hours in the camp escaped my memory.

I was left with a mixture of images: bathing in the communal showers with strange women and children, hours of standing in front of the registration office trying to find out where Bruno and Carlota were, and troubled sleep on the hard iron bed in the intense cold. What I mainly remember is the muffled pain in the pit of my stomach—the pain of parting with my son, the pain of fear that, in days to come, would sprout the tumor that would bring on my demise.

Ricardo and Aldo found ways to amuse themselves, the way little children do. Despite the cold and the rags they wore, they integrated with the other kids and spent their time playing with rocks and balls made from rags. Only the constant hunger left a memory that will forever remain etched in their minds.

The velocity at which our lives had changed was incomprehensible. Up until not long before, I had lived my life as if inside one of those snow globe souvenirs that freeze a picturesque scene, and then the Nazis came, shattering the glass globe into smithereens and trampling all over the blessed routine of the "Princes of the House of Biella" that we were.

The hunger and detachment I felt were horrid, but the worst of it was the uncertainty I had regarding Bruno and Carlota's fate. I made a pact with God, that if Bruno came back, I would say the *Shma Israel* every night and each morning I woke up and added into the bargain my obligation to do a good deed each day until the day I died. The thought of the good deeds I'd do made the anticipation easier.

On the fourth day of our stay at the camp, with still no sign from Bruno and Carlota, Maurizio managed with the help of a little money he gave to one of the clerks, to exit the camp. His plan, which he organized beforehand with Michelangelo, was to contact the Lisco family, our oldest clients whose names I used at the registration office, describing them as our family members. The Lisco family purchased merchandise from us for their textile shop for many years. With the decision to escape to Switzerland, Michelangelo turned to them and, at the same time, created the invitation for Maurizio.

This is how he came to hold a printed invitation to a family event from the Lisco family that arrived by telex. It was clear that the Swiss authorities would also rather we stayed with relatives than in a refugee camp.

And so, when Maurizio left for the "family event," he went to see the family, explained the situation and received their consent for us to stay with them in the attic—two kids and a maid, together with the two of us as a workforce. He arranged with them in advance that we would arrive with two children, and planned to send Bruno to boarding school. According to the strict regulations regarding refugees in Switzerland, the family had to submit a fully detailed formal request in order to "absorb" us. Maurizio helped as much as was needed, and at the same time, each time he went out, he looked in the border events log for Bruno and Carlota, and worse, he looked for evidence of Germans who captured people on the border.

During the next few days, Maurizio kept going out and in again. He patrolled the other refugee camps around, looking for traces of Bruno and Carlota. Every night, when he returned, the camp dwellers would surround him, trying to obtain pieces of information about what was going on in the world. Maurizio became the refugees' foreign minister. They all knew I was waiting for my eldest son, and with the solidarity of rags-wearing refugees, they tried to strengthen my spirit. My prayers didn't seem to change reality, and the sight of Maurizio's hunched shoulders made clear what he didn't have to say in words.

The days went by agonizingly slow. I gave my share of kitchen work to camp's life, and each day, I stole an extra piece of bread hoping to give it to Bruno when he arrived with Maurizio. With each day that passed, my anxiety continued to rise together with the stolen pieces of bread I hid in our room.

In the camp, there were quite a few children that came in through a difficult route, and with no family, and their presence only intensified my concern for Bruno. I tried to remember his smile, but all that I could see was his tearful eyes on the night we parted. I stacked food for him, but the food rotted, and he did not come. Life in the camp became a nightmarish routine. The Swiss were indeed courteous but lacked the patience or the empathy for our situation. The sense of helplessness as refugees was made worse by Bruno and Carlota's absence.

Since our escape, I had heard nothing of the fate of my whole family. They all escaped on foot from Italy to Switzerland, and we didn't know who was all right and who wasn't. The worry for Mother, Celeste and Alberto would not let go. The horror and the pain manifested physically, but my yearning for Bruno threatened my sanity.

Gli Occhi Affamati
(Hungry Eyes)

On the third of March, exactly two months and two days since we had arrived at the camp, I sat outside our shack, not far from the fence close to the office. I would sit there for hours, staring at the gate, and imagine how I would see them arriving. Many refugees came through the gate, but Bruno and Carlota were not among them.

It started to get dark, and the first snowflakes started floating through the air. Ricardo and Aldo played with a ball made of rags near the camp's gate. Beyond the mist of my sadness, I heard Ricardo crying but did not have the mental strength to look at him. Only when the crying stopped abruptly, I lifted my eyes. Someone was talking to my kids that stood next to the gate. I recognized that voice immediately; it was Carlota's voice. But in the thickening darkness, I did not recognize the small figure wrapped in a gray coat. Then it hit me; it was the coat I had given to Carlota before we escaped to the mountains. Carlota herself looked small and thin like a girl. Maurizio walked behind her holding the hand of a boy. For a moment, I wasn't sure it was Bruno. He had a terrified look on his face; he held on tightly to Maurizio's hand and looked like he had shrunk. His clothes were filthy, he was crouching, and his legs barely carried him. My heart was about to burst. I was struggling to move myself toward them, and the stream of tears that had already dried returned gushing from my eyes. Ricardo and Aldo, who stopped their game, ran to me asking, "*Que che?*" and I only mumbled, "Bruno. Bruno. Bruno."

They entered the camp straight into the office, and Maurizio took a long time in there as the camp was very full, and they were not allowing any more people in. Also, Carlota had a strange "correction" in her passport.

I took Ricardo and Aldo by the hand to our room, made the beds and made sure it was obvious that in there it was cozy. I remember the sense of amok with which I cleaned the room, the time that did not pass, and returning to wait for them on the bench outside the office.

When they finally emerged, I jumped on him and sat him in my lap hugging him. The smell of fear mixed together with Bruno's scent. His body was cold and rigid. His hands were freezing, his eyes were moist, and his gaze was dark. I felt him trembling in my arms for quite a while and held him tight. Slowly, the tremor stopped, but his body remained cold and stiff.

At night, I slept next to him, holding him and breathing him in. His bones were sticking out; his thinness was obvious, his soul was crying out in between his interrupted breaths. In the morning, after his first shower and wearing the clothes I gathered for him, I saw how much he had matured in his eyes, and got smaller in size. He had such a profound sadness in his eyes that caused me to keep tearing up. If I could stop time, and go to a moment in the past, I would choose the moment it was decided we would split up, and decide not to. And if they gave me another moment, I would choose the first morning at the refugee camp, when we sat in the dining hall together with our three children and Carlota.

I was grateful to Carlota and able to love Maurizio again. And for a short while, in the refugee camp in Switzerland, I was happy. The mixture of languages sounded from all the tables around us was like beautiful music to my ears, and my stomach—that ailed me so during the days Maurizio kept me apart from Bruno—finally settled.

Maurizio tried to joke, took out a can of sardines from his coat pocket and gave it to us. "I have a fish pond in my stomach," he explained to the boys. The sardine cans were a celebration in honor of Bruno returning to us.

Pianto
(Crying)

After that morning when I woke up with my three children by my side, life at the camp suddenly became bearable.

Up until then, my communication with Maurizio, who was looking for Bruno among the many camps, was summed up by looks. Slowly, resentment started to build up inside me. I did not blame Maurizio; I blamed the war, but I could not understand how he could live with himself after deciding to separate Bruno from us. His practical unremorseful behavior awakened anger in me that I could not voice. I did not allow myself to express my anger. Dark thoughts went through my head, and fear paralyzed me.

I was able to talk to him again, but even then, we didn't view reality in the same way. Maurizio saw ten-and-a-half-year-old Bruno as an adult for all intents and purposes; I saw him as a child, a child that needed me.

I heard the story about what happened during the days after we separated in Como from Carlota.

She said the night they passed the border was cold and dark. They found the opening in the fence quite easily and then they marched with Carlota holding his hand. From a distance, they could hear the barking of German dogs, and with every step they took, they could hear the leaves moving under the soles of the shoes. It started snowing, and the mist had a soothing effect on their walk. They marched through the woods in the severe cold with a ten-year-old boy holding the hand of a thirty-year-old woman. They couldn't see the view, and the distant barking of dogs intensified the fear they felt.

It was already 5 a.m. They had been walking for more than two hours trying to distance themselves from the border. Everything was gray around them. Carlota, who during her childhood went on hikes with her family in the mountains of Italy, knew that there should be a cabin in the woods where the hunters and the rangers kept their tools, and in stormy weather even found shelter in them. She thought that maybe they, too, could find shelter until the day cleared up. All of a sudden, the dogs and the German language sounded closer. Bruno and Carlota looked at one another and started to run hand in hand, in the fog, to distance themselves. The sun already began to shine, and the frozen still Swiss forest seemed like it wondered what the hastiness and fuss was all about. When they grew short of breath from running through the cold air, they paused and looked around.

In the background, they heard Germans shouting and what sounded like a moving car not far from them. Carlota pointed at an uprooted tree that had a hole next to it and said in a whisper, "Bruno, we'll hide here until they pass."

He entered the hole without saying a word and helped her pull the branches on top of it to cover it. He then sat down on the icy ground and Carlota, who had three pieces of bread in her pocket, gave Bruno two and ate one herself. Michelangelo gave her those three pieces at the meeting place, minutes before they climbed into the truck.

And so, as they were sitting in the pit in the woods, silently chewing on their bread at this bizarre picnic, the barking of the dogs, the metal rattle of weapons, and loud voices speaking in German came closer and closer. The breath sounds of the approaching dogs were what Carlota heard the clearest—dogs and metal. Those noises, she said as she described those moments to me, would haunt her dreams for years to come.

A dog paused near the pit, barking. Carlota mumbled a prayer to Jesus, and Bruno's body froze without movement. After an unknown period of time, the dog's breath sounds moved away followed by an echoing gunshot, after which everything became dead silent. Bruno's tears were pouring out of his eyes without a sound, and Carlota was crying, too. Carlota couldn't tell me how long they sat like that in silence. When they rose from the pit, they were soaking wet from the ground, the snow that penetrated the leaves, as well as fear.

In the morning light, they could see the abandoned hunter's cabin quite clearly. Carlota pulled dry socks from her coat for her and Bruno and suggested he lay on the bench that was there. She covered him with her coat, and he fell asleep.

She sat there in the cabin, safeguarding Bruno as he slept, while every rustle of leaves made her jump. After a few hours, when it started to get dark, they went on the road again, and as they reached the paved road, Swiss soldiers captured them and put them on a truck. Michelangelo explained to them that, should they be picked up by Swiss soldiers, no harm will come to them. The same had been explained to us as well.

I recall how I sat with Carlota on a bench in the camp when she told me this story. It was outside the dining hall, and the whole time, I kept hearing the footsteps of people walking on gravel.

"When the soldiers captured us," Carlota told me, "I was glad. Finally, this nightmare in the mountains was over. But later on, I saw that something about the Swiss was a lot like the Germans."

A tough Swiss policewoman and a soldier drove them to a detention center. It was already evening, but no one paid any attention to them. They were left hungry and nervous in some room as soldiers were coming in and out. At some point, one of the soldiers told them that they would soon be brought before a judge.

"We were moved to a larger, colder room," Carlota said, "and then we heard the sound of a big car stopping outside, and through the window, we saw a man wearing a robe and two other men coming out of the car. In the meantime, they organized the room we were put in into some kind of an improvised courtroom. After a while, they brought us into the room and sat us down together for a speedy trial. The policewoman who brought us to the detention center handed our documents to the robe-wearing judge, and I saw him feeling our passports, checking them from side to side. Bruno sat completely still.

"I panicked. I hoped they wouldn't say our passports were fake. Suddenly, the police officers brought a few more refugees into the room. I heard the word *Chicoslovaky*. There were five of them, all wearing rags, emitting a foul odor—a pretty girl and a full-bodied woman that was hugging three small children. After a few minutes, the judge sentenced them to be deported and ordered they'd be escorted out of the room. The Swiss police officers handled them harshly and ignored the heartbreaking cries of the full-bodied woman. I looked at Bruno and saw the fear in his eyes. He looked small and shrunken.

"Our name was called. We stood up, and the judge, with a serious look on his face, asked Bruno in Italian where he was from. Bruno answered in Italian that he was from Biella and that he did not know where his parents were or what happened to them, and only I was with him. Then the judge asked who I was to him, and Bruno said, 'She is a friend of my mother's, my mother is gone,' and started crying."

"The judge moved in his chair in unease, and I stood up and apologized, and I told him that the family was separated when the Germans came into Biella, and Bruno, who found himself alone came to me and told me, then together, we escaped to the mountains. The judge looked in my passport again and said, 'You will probably go back to Italy.' I told him I couldn't leave this child here on his own, and that he had relatives here. I promised that, once I reunited him with his relatives, I would return to Italy.

"All this time, Bruno didn't stop crying. I never saw him cry like that before. His whole body was shaking.

"The judge left the room, and the guards all watched how I approached Bruno with a used handkerchief, giving it to him to blow his nose. After a few minutes, the judge returned and gave us visas to stay in Switzerland. The policewoman escorted us to the jeep that took us to a transitional refugee camp."

"My mother is gone." This sentence, that brought my son back to me, made me thank God. I hugged Bruno and whispered in his ear, "You are a hero."

I remember myself sitting on the bench, chilled to the bone, listening to Carlota's story, how he cried and touched the judge's heart by telling him that he had no one in the world except her. And I thanked the Lord and Bruno for having the courage to cry. Bruno's cry and his fear were what kept him and Carlota together.

That sentence—"My mother is gone"—stayed with me night and day. I told Maurizio, who ignored the sad parts and complimented Bruno, in front of his brothers, about his ability to survive.

They stayed in the transitional camp for a few weeks, and Carlota managed to keep Bruno with her. She gave the few coins that were sewn into her coat's lining to the guard at the entrance to the camp, and told him he would receive more if he told *Señor* Vitale, when he came looking for his son that he was there.

Maurizio, who passed through the camps looking for Bruno, arrived there and found him, and the guard to whom Carlota gave the coins, indeed received more coins as Carlota promised.

I, who prayed and worried, who made a vow to God if Bruno came back, realized that there was a God and he was with me. Now that Bruno was back, and the huge knot of anxiety that was inside me for many long weeks had dissipated, I decided to uphold the vow I took to perform one good deed each day. I did not skip a day. People were amazed at the sight of half an apple, a slice of bread, or a towel. Everything I could give, I gave. I performed good deeds inside the camp and out of the camp as well. I felt that it was what brought Bruno back to me. The truth is I knew all along, that every good deed I had done, paled in comparison with Carlota's sacrifice. Carlota kept him safe, sacrificing her identity for him. She, by her sheer existence, was my teacher.

Rilassamento
(Short Comfort)

My two little boys, Aldo and Ricardo, clung to Bruno and hugged him. They both survived the camp well. At times, it even seemed sane. Michelangelo returned to haunt my dreams, appeared and didn't let go. With a beard, without a beard, as a young youth like when I first met him, and even as he was at the time Maurizio was in Ethiopia. I didn't confide these dreams to Maurizio.

In no time, the "forces" between Maurizio and me were equal. Even inside the walls of the camp, he was still the same wise and authoritative man I knew. Before two weeks had passed since Bruno arrived, we knew that in the next few weeks we would be allowed to leave the camp to visit the Lisco family. Maurizio came back with their consent and whispered in my ear, "We will have an attic there, and you and Carlota will help out around the house. I am trying to find myself something to do there to earn a living. We will leave the two little ones with us and search for a boarding school for Bruno."

"Let's take him with us," I said, and the words "I have no one in the world" echoed in my ears. But Maurizio was determined. Bruno was already a big boy, almost eleven. He, too, had been sent to a boarding school in England at the age of fourteen, where he studied two years of high school and two years of textile studies. Maurizio remembered the boarding school as a constitutive and good experience. It was interesting, and it was there he met his lifelong friend, Havkin. But Bruno was only eleven and didn't even look as old as that. On the contrary, his growth seemed to have stopped. It was obvious that hunger scared him. He walked around camp like a shadow and ate whatever he could at every opportunity.

Maurizio believed Bruno would be better off with kids his own age so he could learn, evolve. I only wanted him next to me. I did everything I could think of to prevent him from sending Bruno away. I promised I would teach him Latin every day, if only he would stay near me. Maurizio claimed I was a spoiling mother, and that all I wanted was to hinder Bruno's growth. He continued his efforts to locate a boarding school in the area that would be willing to accept Bruno but was unsuccessful. One of the Lisco relatives suggested a boarding school in Veve, which was about an eight-hour train ride away, near the French border. I prayed they had no openings. I felt as if we were playing a game of roulette with our lives. We managed to escape twice somehow, and now, when we were together again and could leave the camp, why send Bruno away, and tempt his fate?

But it was impossible to talk to Maurizio about it. He did not believe in fate. Everything had to be rational with him. He was adamant and claimed that Bruno's future was more important, and those were the years he should be studying and not be with us.

During all of our conversations I remembered wishing to say to Maurizio, "But you were wrong once before you thought that the war will not reach us, not touch us. How do you know now that you are right?"

I didn't. I let him go and come back. I collected used clothes that would fit Bruno like a good refugee, made sure he ate, that he gained a little more weight, hugged him, slept next to him knowing he wanted me near him, and that he understood we wanted what's best for him.

Today, when I try to recall what I was thinking then, I remember that each time, the thought of having to part with Bruno again brought tears to my eyes. I stopped thinking and performed like a machine.

A week later, the confirmation of Bruno's registration to boarding school came, and Maurizio also returned with the permits he obtained for all of us to leave the camp and stay with the Lisco family.

I didn't know whether to rejoice or be saddened by the fact he was able to do so much. Every time, he came back with another "achievement," I found myself wondering about the amount of things a man can do outside his home base. I ask myself now that I am sick, what would Maurizio do? Would he have taken me to America to consult the finest doctors? Would he travel with me to Italy and take me hiking in the mountains?

Maurizio changed during the war, and following his change, I was forced to change, too. The balance between us was broken. He was wrong. We did not prepare correctly and paid for this mistake by running around like a madman. He altered his thinking. The moment he was disappointed by the Italians and in a way from the Swiss, as well, he decided as the war was raging, that we would not stay in Europe.

In hindsight, I think it was what held him together and gave him the strength to face me with my worried looks and dark thoughts, to handle the rumors arriving from everywhere in Europe, and to face our daily life at the camp with the non-edible food and many other refugees from all around Italy and Europe. As if he "connected" to a vision, and the day-to-day life had no obstacles in his eyes. It seemed all he could see was the future. It looked like that to him, the more he planned into the future, the faster the time would go by, and the war would end.

In many aspects, we became closer during the war, but we also grew apart because we didn't view Bruno in the same manner. Parting with Bruno devastated me; he was strengthened by it.

The thought of sending Bruno to boarding school was followed by the knowledge that once the war was over, Bruno would need to find his place in the world, and Maurizio did not want him to miss any more school. He also explained to me, in the little we talked after sending Bruno away to school, that keeping Bruno with us would have been like surrendering to the Germans and halting his life. Maurizio did not recognize surrender. The mere fact he existed in a refugee camp away from his business was in his eyes a form of surrender he barely lived with.

Eventually, I gave in to the boarding school idea without fully knowing what it really meant. Today when I think of those days, I get chills. How could such a small child travel so far on his own?! But then—when life in ten days felt like living a year and you didn't know where your family members were—the thought that it could be pleasant for him made me cooperate. I pictured him playing tennis on the lawns with other children his age.

And so, about two and a half weeks after our reunion, even before all the gold coins were unpicked from his coat, Bruno was put on a train again, this time, without Carlota to save him. I cried bitterly again; his little brothers seemed happier than him again.

I went with him and Maurizio to the train station in Bellinzona to see him off. Bellinzona was a picturesque Swiss town that looked then like a war-town occupying many soldiers and masses of refugees.

We stood on the platform of the train to Veve, and Bruno looked shrunken and grim. I could tell he was scared and knew there was nothing I could possibly do in front of Maurizio. I tried to hug him, and he evaded me, telling me "I don't want to."

I told him, "It's a good boarding school; you will like it a lot. We will come to visit you, and on your birthday, you'll be with us." I spoke but did not believe myself. The tears choked me, and Maurizio kept silent.

His mustache trembled a little; he embraced Bruno, kissed him on the head and put him in the cart. We hugged, and parted.

Collegio
(Boarding School)

I found out a few months later, that Bruno became gravely ill immediately upon arriving at the boarding school.

The journey lasted a day and a half, during which he felt sick the whole time, with only older children he did not know around him. The school nurse that came to check the new arrivals touched his forehead and noticed he was burning with fever. Bruno was left in the infirmary. Vinegar compresses were placed on his forehead and limbs, but nothing helped. He was burning up and feeling terrible. After two days in the school's infirmary, he was rushed to the Veve hospital, where he was diagnosed with Scarlet Fever.

This diagnosis sentenced him to a month in isolation in the hospital. The nurse came in only once a day, bringing a plate of food. This was a harsh verdict for a child of not yet eleven—to be in hospital, during the war, alone, hearing nothing but a foreign language around him. The entire time, I thought Bruno was studying and having fun. I wrote him letters and anticipated a reply. It was two months later that we received the bill from the hospital he was in.

The war created havoc with one's inner emotions. I silenced

the voices within that called for a decisive refusal to another parting with Bruno. I obeyed everything Maurizio said. He said boarding school was great for children, and it was where lifelong friends were made. I found it convenient. I wanted to believe it was true. To think that all this time, Bruno was in the hospital, while I imagined him singing songs in French and playing soccer on the grass with children his own age.

At that time, we moved in with a family that agreed to take us n, The Lisco family. Carlota stayed with us. Her passport presented her false identity as Jewish. Maurizio managed to secure a position in the offices of *Ferband*, which was a Jewish organization in Switzerland. He now had a reason to get up in the morning, and it provided a little income that enabled us to assist the kind family who housed us in the attic.

We stayed with the Lisco family for many long months. At first, we meticulously hid in the rat-infested attic in fear of the neighbors and the authorities, but soon our papers were organized. Mr. Lisco declared that we relatives who arrived from Italy should assist with the family business. After that, we climbed to the attic only at nightfall. In order not to bother our gracious hosts, I made sure the children used the bathroom only in the morning when the Lisco's were out of the house.

We hardly stepped into the spacious living room. The heavy wooden furniture, the floral upholstery and the fine chinaware in the dark sideboard Mrs. Lisco inherited from her grandmother, awakened the sorrow and yearning I had for my light and spacious living room, for my crystal vases and the soft cotton curtains.

Carlota and I spent many hours in the kitchen. She would iron, and I made my homemade tomato and basil sauce.

I can barely remember the eight months we lived with the Lisco family in Switzerland. I remember Aldo and Ricardo were always at my side, Carlota praying, and Maurizio traveling back and forth to Zurich. I also remember the terrifying moments when we heard the rumor that London, too, was bombarded, and yet Hitler refused to end the war.

Relative to what we heard was happening in Europe, especially to Jews, we were very lucky. We were in Switzerland, safe.

But throughout the time from the night we escaped our home, I had a hole in my stomach. Slowly, my hips started to shrink, and Maurizio's gaze stopped lingering on it. The entire time I had dark thoughts and yearnings that ached in my bones. In my dreams, Michelangelo and Napoleon roamed the camps together with ghosts, bringing food to Bruno.

I recall not being able to fall asleep for many nights. I would walk around in a daze, hearing Aldo tossing in his bed, hearing the mice squeak, knowing that our fortune was relatively good because there were Jews freezing to death in labor camps. When I finally managed to sleep, Bruno's eyes were looking at me helplessly. I bestowed all the love and guilt I felt on Ricardo and Aldo, who learned to play soccer and read next to the chickens in the Lisco family's barn. I tried not to lose my mind and dreamt of how we would go back to our lives in Biella.

Here is how Maurizio described what we were going through in a letter he dictated to me for his friend in London,

Arthur Havkin. But before that, I have to disclose how I came into possession of these letters.

Our correspondence with Maurizio's friend from his time at the London College was a beacon of sanity for us during the war. Havkin was corresponding at the same time with Alberto and Emanuelle, as well as with Michelangelo, and was, in fact, a center of information for the whole family, and fortunately a source for transferring funds. Emanuelle would send us money from America through Havkin, and he, in turn, would transfer the funds to us inside books and newspapers.

Havkin's letters recently found their way to me with my granddaughter Irit, when she returned from London. When I re-read them, I realized they more or less reflected the situation we were in, at least as Maurizio saw it anyway.

A letter to Havkin—11th of May, 1944—

(Maurizio dictated, and I typed it on the typewriter at the Lisco's house):

"My dear Arthur,

"It's been five months since we escaped Italy. Up until now, we were in a Swiss camp, and it was thanks to the Swiss Lisco family's guarantee (half Italian and half Swiss), that we were released to their home and at present, are in Winterthur: Vittoria, Ricardo, Aldo, and myself. Bruno is in a French-Swiss college on the other side of Switzerland. *Nonna* Josephina, Alberto, and his family are in Locarno. Alberto and his wife Elsa escaped, and made a decision at first to leave the girls Nora and Silvia in an orphanage in Italy, but we have lately learned that his wife's parents got them across the border and that Silvia became sick. Now the whole family is reunited in Locarno. Alberto managed to survive as a public restroom janitor in Locarno.

"In a postcard we received from him, he wrote, 'I clean... and get to use it first.' At least, he didn't lose his sense of humor. We hadn't heard from Michelangelo for a long time, and I think he is probably in a labor camp in Bern. I presume you heard about Aunt Ada, from the condolences we received. I hope that you and your family are well and that you managed to avoid the war and its injustice. Are you still in Caruso? I am not sure you are there. I am sending the letter to London and hope it reaches you in time.

"So far, I haven't succeeded in receiving any news regarding Emanuelle, but a letter came from the committee that handles the refugees, saying that my brother sent money for us. If by any chance, you know what is happening in America, we would be most curious to learn what is happening with Lina, Emanuelle's wife that was due to give birth by the end of January, and since then, we have been unable to contact them. My mother is with Alberto, and from them, we do receive letters every now and again. One day or another, we must get together. We should meet again like we did in Italy and in England before the war. Then we can talk about the problems caused by the war. Please excuse my poor English, I haven't used it much for some time now; I have almost forgotten it. I think that you are working too much, but I hope it will all be over by the end of the year. Kisses to your mother, Lilly, and to Sonia, your sister. Vittoria sends her regards".

Ubergassa 22, Winterthur."

While we stayed at the Lisco house in Winterthur, we wrote Bruno at the boarding school, but we rarely received a reply from him. The few letters we did receive were short and in the form of a report. It was clear that someone in school was reading what he wrote. In one of the letters, he informed us that on his birthday, he would come to visit. I waited for six months to see my son. Train stations always remind me of that meeting.

I stood in the Zurich Grand Station with Maurizio and Carlota, who was overwhelmed by the mayhem. Thousands of uniform-wearing people filled the hall—German officers, Swiss policemen, and the Allied Forces were mixed together with many people carrying packages. I just stood there, firmly holding Carlota's hand. My heart was about to burst with excitement as the train pulled into the station. Foggy smoke came off the tracks and the doors opened with a loud screeching sound. Passengers carrying suitcases came off the train and fell with excitement on the shoulders of relatives waiting for them. Cries of joy and sobbing sounded all around.

We looked around, searching for Bruno's figure, but we couldn't see him anywhere. Terror gripped my throat, a quick look into Maurizio's eyes made it clear that his thoughts were also nightmarish. "The boy isn't here."

The station started to empty; the train doors slammed shut in a loud noise and steam came up from the tracks again. The three of us stood there, glued to our spot, when out of the steamy fog of the disappearing train, approached a small figure with a suitcase, striding slowly, heavily. I wasn't sure it was him, and the memory of not recognizing my son right away was and still is unbearable, and never goes away. I hurried and ran to him, my heels clicking loudly on the empty platform. I was breathing heavily. He stopped in his tracks, set his heavy suitcase down and looked at us with a vacant gaze. Carlota, who was behind us, called out his name, and Bruno waved at her tiredly. He did not smile. He just stood there, limp, with a pale face, and his wide-open eyes merely emphasized the dark circles around them. He looked so thin and small, his suit hanging on him as if he had dressed up in his father's clothes. When I hugged him, his eyes welled up. Without saying a word, we paced toward the platform of the train to Winterthur, with Carlota carrying the suitcase as I held on tightly to Bruno's hand. The train station was bustling all around us as we walked with a heavy silence between us. Maurizio was waiting for us under the station's clock, smiling a smile of relief. He patted Bruno on his back and spoke to him in French. Bruno did not answer.

We made our way to Winterthur from Zurich together, three adults trying to assess the damage caused to this silent boy at our side. Maurizio tried to encourage him to talk, this time in Italian and Bruno described in carefully chosen words a cold and unpleasant place, in which he was sick most of the time. He found the French learning very hard, and the sores on his hands were a living testimony to the ruler spanking he received each time he pronounced wrong. There was something about being a mother who is unable to sense what is happening to her so that makes one feel disabled. It felt like a punch to my stomach. My stomach turned—a mother who feels nothing. This whole time that I had pictured him

playing soccer and tennis with his friends on a green lawn
or on a clay court, he was being smacked on his hands and
placed in quarantine as he got sick again and again.

The birthday celebration, which the little ones waited
impatiently for, was quite sad. Bruno was too hungry to eat
and too depressed to talk. He was so fatigued, he fell asleep
immediately.

We ate his birthday cake the next day. During the first few
days, he didn't speak and hardly moved. His wounded fingers
and his wide-open eyes ran shivers down my spine. Carlota
didn't stop making orange juice and trying to entice him with
thick slices of bread smeared with jam. Only with great difficulty and very slowly, did his brothers manage to bring a
smile to his face, but his gaze remained blank. I remember
the weeks in which he slept with us in the mice infested attic
as weeks of horror. We already knew that Jews were being
murdered, we had already exposed Bruno to sickness and
loneliness, and the war was not yet over.

And how did Maurizio see himself for what he did to Bruno
by insisting he went to boarding school to study French?

Another letter to his friend Havkin in London he dictated
to me at the same time Bruno came to us, reflects his position
and feelings on the matter:

11 July 1944

"Dear Arthur,

"This is a great day for me because I received a letter from
you with regards from Emanuelle. I am sorry it took such a
long time and that it was apprehended by the authorities, and I
hope that this letter will reach you within a few days. I had the

good sense and a good feeling about moving to Switzerland. Trying not to think what could have happened to us.

"I can't write to you about all that has happened to us. I hope we will be able to meet soon, and then I will tell you all that has happened. Michelangelo hasn't contacted us for some time now, and we have no clue as to what happened to Vittoria's mother and her father's sister.

"Vittoria's older sister is also in Switzerland. We were lucky to have good people from our past who helped us evade the wrong doings of the Germans in Italy. The whole family is here in Switzerland. Please tell Emanuelle that we are doing well. Emanuelle was wise to send you a letter for us, please tell him we were very happy to receive news from them. I don't know if you received my previous letter I sent you a few months ago. I was saddened to hear your dear mother had passed away. She was nice and smart, and I am sorry for your loss. I will never forget her kindness and generosity. There are rumors here about bombardments in London; I hope you did not suffer any damages to your home and your spectacular paintings. I am looking forward to our next meeting; we are sending you our warmest regards. Bruno is spending his holiday with us after a few months in a French boarding school, and he will spend his birthday with us too. Next week, he will return to college; this time, he will learn Hebrew.

"Ricardo and Aldo send kisses. I promised them that after the war, we will come visit you in London. Vittoria also sends her condolences. I miss you a lot and hope that the war will end soon. Can't wait to see you.

"My warmest regards, Maurizio."

"Bruno is spending his holiday with us after a few months in a French boarding school..." this is how he told his friend, whom he knew from his boarding school days in England. Next week, he will return to college; this time, he will learn Hebrew." So simple...

In reality, it was clear to Maurizio too that there was no way Bruno would return to that boarding school, but it was very cramped at the Lisco house, and Maurizio, who had already learned Hebrew himself, wanted to send him to a Jewish boarding school where Jewish studies, Torah and Hebrew were learned. That boarding school, which was part of the world *Mizrahi* movement, was Maurizio's solution that he got from his contacts with the "New Jews." He promised Bruno that it would only be for a few months until the war ended, and Bruno accepted.

My resistance was futile. I barely agreed to listen to Maurizio and Carlota, who claimed that we needed to create an experience of a good boarding school for Bruno if he was ever going to get over the trauma of the French boarding school. All of my instincts screamed against it, but I was helpless to resist.

Today, I think that all the strength I had later in life, was a reaction to the helplessness I felt during the war.

Il Suicidio Di Hitler
(Hitler Committed Suicide)

"Hitler committed suicide," Maurizio's voice thundered as he stormed through the door waving a newspaper. It was dinner-time in the kitchen of the Lisco family. Maurizio sat down with the paper in his hands and told us of the group of Jews he met at the train station. They came from the *Fossoli*[5] concentration camp, from which their families were deported to Auschwitz in Poland. They survived that fate and came home, thin as skeletons, dressed in rags, their eyes blank, and they had no one in the world. They didn't even have a home to go back to.

"Transitional camps will be erected, after which all the Jewish refugees will immigrate to the country of Israel on boats that will be purchased, with the assistance of the Jewish

---

5   The Fossoli concentration camp was erected in the north of Italy, not far from Venice in May of 1942 and was used as a prisoners of war camp. From the invasion of the Nazi army into Italy in December 1943 until their departure from Italy in August 1944, the camp was used as a concentration camp for Jews, from which about 2500 Italian Jews were shipped by trains to Auschwitz.

Agency. Europe is closed to those who wish to exit it, but there will be no recourse. Jews cannot remain in Europe; they need to go to Palestine, that's the place!" Maurizio's voice thundered, and I was horrified by the description and mumbled a prayer of thanks for our good fortune.

Maurizio started telling us about the camps. After months of trying to spare the kids information about the horrors, he spoke openly about them as the room became completely silent. I did not dare utter a word to him.

In fact, there was no way to conceal the reality from the children even if it was unconceivable. They perceived it anyway with their keen senses. That war was pure evil. From behind the elegant façade of the German culture, emerged cruelty unknown to the human race before. Maurizio would return from his meetings pale and hunched whispering in my ear the atrocious stories he heard from the refugees who survived the camps on Polish land.

The pain threatening to kill me today was born then, at the moment I thought of Bruno, who was alone at the boarding school, and how he could have been taken from there very easily to go up in the oven's smoke.

In retrospect, I don't understand how I did that. I can't explain to myself how I agreed to leave him alone and far away for the duration of that war. I wish he would have thrown the question of "How did you leave me? How could you agree?" in my face. But he didn't.

He doesn't ask. He isn't angry.

The news that the Allied Forces were about to finally defeat Germany quickly became reality, and I started planning our return to Biella with Carlota. As far as Maurizio was concerned, Biella was supposed to be a transitional station only. He was adamant to emigrate to Palestine with all of us including Carlota, and he drove me and the kids insane when he forced us to learn Hebrew, that difficult foreign language.

I played along, hoping that when we returned to Biella, to the warehouses, home, family, the *Castello*, he would let it go. But Maurizio was determined in his decision to leave Europe.

On our last night in Switzerland, he lay beside me, holding my hand, and enthusiastically whispered his dreams in my ear. His brown eyes blazed with passion, his cheeks were glistening—his vitality had returned to him.

Dopo La Guerra
(After the War)

The next morning, with trains loaded with refugees moving to the length and breadth of Europe like swarms of ants, we left the Lisco house for the train station to catch the train home. Bruno was waiting for us at the station, thin and silent with fringes (*Tsisit*—a Jewish four corner garment) hanging from his clothes.

I remember the long train ride to Biella, Maurizio's attempts to get him to talk, Bruno's short and evasive answers, and Maurizio mumbling, "He doesn't know French, and very little Hebrew. How will he study for his *Bar Mitzvah*?"

My eyes filled with tears of frustration. I knew the problem wasn't the fact he didn't know the language, but alienation, the strangeness that now existed between us and our first born. I wanted to throw in Maurizio's face, "You see? He would have been better off with us, at least he would have known Italian, and how to hug." But I kept silent. As usual, I was quiet.

The trip back to Biella from Switzerland was the first time I noticed the physical resemblance between Maurizio and Bruno. They both remained immersed in their thoughts. Maurizio already updated us that Biella hadn't changed, but our business was robbed, and all of our merchandise was stolen. Bruno seemed as if he was robbed of his soul, terrified of the unknown that awaited us. We had so many expectations for him, for this young boy at the end of the war, I expected him to smile, Carlota expected him to eat, and Maurizio expected him to be an honor student.

Surprisingly enough, Bruno met all of them. I have told him everything now. I know that soon I will not be here, and there are some subjects I cannot avoid talking about.

I will never forget the first phone call to Lina after the war. I closed the door to Maurizio's study; shaking, I dialed her number, and as soon as I heard her uplifting "Hello, *pronto*," I burst into tears and sobbed for over an hour. I cried for the yearning, the mental damage I thought I had caused Bruno and myself, the financial devastation and destruction we found upon our return, for the panic I felt facing Maurizio's dreams about the country of Israel, and for the severed bond between my first born and me that would probably never heal.

From Lina, I heard about the good life she had with Emanuelle, that he was earning a good living, and that they had just purchased a spacious new apartment and nice furniture.

Anna was already attending school, and Lina had American friends that got together to play cards. Sami (named after Samuelle) and Alfred were growing up, and she wasn't sure they would ever return to Italy, but soon, when it was possible, they would come for a visit.

Traveling from America to Italy wasn't simple because of the war.

We discussed our letter correspondence made possible with the help of Havkin in London, and I told her about Aldo and Ricardo. I did not tell her though about the poverty, the fuel shortage and that nothing was left in the warehouse. I didn't tell her about our workers that allowed the looting to happen, and of how betrayed we felt in our hometown. I did not disclose that every time Maurizio talked about Palestine, Michelangelo would look at me to check my reaction, and, sure enough, I didn't tell her that sometimes, he appeared in my dreams. I did not tell her about the look on the faces of the refugees from the camp near Biella, and nothing about the pain I had in my stomach.

There are certain things you can't talk about during a phone conversation. I found myself telling her quite proudly that Maurizio came back from the war with renewed strengths as if he slept for an entire year. That he was working day in and day out on all fronts, rushing to suppliers, obtaining credit and buying merchandise, running to clients to let them know we were back, that he set up a school for Bruno and got Aldo and Ricardo into first grade. I told her that I was trying, between taking care of my home and going to the office, to keep my vows and do good deeds.

All the children were there, all relatively healthy. All of my sisters were alive, and so were Maurizio's brothers. Someone was indeed watching over us. Aunt Celeste passed away immediately after they returned to Vercelli, leaving my mother on her own, but something about running away and coming back made her younger and more vital, and she wished us to get together.

Returning to Biella after the war was difficult. Our front door had been breached and was wide open, the drawers were open, and hardly any silver was left, or towels or linen. Nothing of value remained. My father's picture was left out of the frame it was in, and I couldn't find Samuelle's photograph.

The neighbors, who throughout our lives had been a part of it, turned a cold shoulder. Despair filled my heart. I didn't feel at home; I didn't feel safe. Our neighbors, who allowed this to happen, were possibly part of the looting, and it was only the beginning. Nothing was left of our business, and yet, I was happy to come home. The Germans were gone; I was able to sleep in my own bed and prepare our own food.

Carlota and I stormed the house, scrubbing every corner, renewing all that was missing from our kitchen, and finding solace.

During the war, my soul became bound to Carlota's. She became my closest friend and a sister like the one I missed terribly. We spent many hours having heart-to-heart conversations over pots of pasta and trays of dehydrated tomatoes.

Those are the moments I miss the most. I will never forget her love and devotion. When Aldo traveled to Italy, he promised me he'd buy Carlota the chocolate she loved. Just thinking about her brings me to tears.

I remember our first meeting with Michelangelo after the war. I was home, and I heard his footsteps, surprised at my pounding heart. I passed by the mirror and saw myself blushing.

"Carlota," I called her, "look who's here" as I opened the door. Tall, bearded, strong and smiling he hugged me.

"I was at the office," he said. "I was surprised not to see you there." I thought to myself he probably missed me, too, and so, without explicitly saying it, he brought Maurizio into the room. Carlota and the boys arrived at the entrance hall and managed to make my embarrassment, blushing and looks disappear.

The boys jumped on him as always, as Michelangelo was like a brother to them, and they loved him with all their hearts.

Michelangelo matured and grew wider during the war. He kept his contacts with the people in the resistance and always carried a weapon. As opposed to him, Maurizio acted as if he had turned his back on Italy. He insisted on talking Hebrew in the house, and the main topic of conversation was Palestine and emigrating there. Be it as it may, their brotherly love was not hindered in the least, and Michelangelo, with his reddish beard and gray eyes, resumed his visits, back to having meals with us, and every now and again, brought a beautiful girl with him to decorate our dinner table.

The post-war Biella was slightly bruised but felt like home again.

The shop windows looked like they were frozen in time, but the flowers bloomed, and nice aromas came up from the coffee shops. In the streets, women were seen in their pant-yhose and heels, waiting for the men to pick them up for a date, and kissing them on street corners.

"As long as there are couples kissing in the world, there is a chance that life will return to what it used to be," Michelangelo used to tease me whenever I complained about the shortage of butter, fuel, customers, money, or Maurizio's time.

Routine E L'Amore
(Routine and Love)

Maurizio returned to look at me again, to fondle me and to whisper words in my ear. He insisted on saying his words of love in Hebrew. He was different now from the man I married. From a spoiled rich kid with a well-groomed mustache, he became a Zionist activist with a vision. His hair and mustache started to show streaks of gray, and two more wrinkles appeared on his forehead. I asked myself more than once whether I could have fallen in love with this Zionist or with Michelangelo with whom I had an exciting reunion. Having him back in our lives returned him to my dreams. He also had a new occupation.

Not far from Biella, the "Joint," together with the Red Cross and the Jewish Agency, erected a refugee camp. Many among them discovered they had nowhere to return to and wished to go to Palestine to build themselves a new life. Some departed to Palestine on boats without permits and certificates. Maurizio was one of the people who dealt with this illegal emigration. I resented the fact that Maurizio became public. I complained about the fact he was busy less with family matters and more with the refugees, but I loved the path he took when he used his contacts and strengths to promote purchasing the boats or trading food stamps. Michelangelo and Alberto were with him on his mission, and I found myself emptying closets in the house to give clothes to the refugees, cooking pots of food, and buying them cigarettes.

Maurizio did not rest. With all his might he took care of the people at camp PauLina. He recruited the Red Cross, sent flour, oil, and permits. He activated all the lawyers he knew, enlisted anyone he could, and he himself took the clothes I sorted at home to the camp. Toward the weekend, he went to the market to buy fruit and vegetables for Saturday. We cooked vast amounts of food and hosted people at our house who returned from the hell of war.

Each gathering at our house turned into a collection center for camp PauBellina. Every Friday, we drove up to the camp with food and cigarettes to cheer up the thin people gathered there from all over Europe.

"They are all Jews," Maurizio used to say to me, and I admit, I felt that God had put them in my path to give gratitude for my life, to understand how fortunate I was, so I could find a way to live in peace.

Maurizio didn't know and didn't want to know peace. Next to his activities for the refugees, from the time we returned to Biella, he made huge efforts to retrieve our property and rehabilitate it. This was how he described the situation in those days to his friend Arthur Havkin in London, four months after the war was over:

12Th October' 1945

"Dear Arthur,

"It is truly wonderful to read your words and anticipate meeting with you after six years.

"Unfortunately, the situation in Biella is not so good. The Nazis stole 350 Million Italian *Liras* from us. Remember how big the warehouse was? And how huge the factory was? But lives were saved, and that is enough. We are working day and night, trying to put the company back on track, buying and selling, and in a few years, will become one of the largest companies again.

"If you can, please send us good quality wool, from Australia if possible. It will be a good investment. Because our industry is not advancing, we have no raw materials. If you can, approach Leeds and check if we can do business with them. We have assets. The small villa in Bordighera, near Sanremo by the beach is fully furnished, and it has a garden. I am happy to invite you, and I can send you a map. It would be best if you came to visit, so you could see for yourself. We are waiting for the time you will be able to. Bruno is always speaking of you and has already turned into a man. Next summer, I am planning to send him to England to learn English.

"The other two, Aldo and Ricardo want to know who this unknown uncle is, and I can't wait to get on the first plane and bring them to you.

"Things are not too bad. If you are willing to pay the right price, you can get what you need.

"It is better here than in Switzerland, and we are short of nothing. If you have enough money, you can live like a king.

"As you can see, it is quite a long letter. I hope you will understand it because I am not so sure my English is good. I hope that you, your family and all your people are doing well.

"My children send their warmest regards, many kisses, Maurizio."

This letter reminded me that Maurizio also included Havkin in his efforts to renew production in our factory, as well as prepare his next step in grooming Bruno as the family's heir and business successor for the future, by learning English.

It is possible to say that after his terrible fiasco of trying to foresee the future with regard to the war Maurizio developed the gift of foresight. Over the years, he indeed sent Aldo, who already knew English, to study textiles at Leeds University in England. But in the meantime, Bruno was still just a child, and we were getting ready to celebrate his *Bar Mitzvah*. The synagogue in Biella reopened and was bustling with people. The Jewish community, townsfolk like us as well as the refugees, attended. Even those who were never really religious felt at home and in the right place, and now that we understood a little Hebrew, the songs and prayers became a little more meaningful.

In a short time, a *Bar Mitzvah* ceremony was organized for all the children that had returned: our Bruno, Guido, Celeste's son, and Julio (who was fifteen at the time but never got to celebrate his *Bar Mitzvah*), and three more children from the refugee camp. They were all called up to read in the Torah, all studied with the rabbi, and they were all thankful for the privilege.

We women sat on the second story of the synagogue— Carlota, who hid her crucifix under her shirt and sat proudly watching Bruno sing in Hebrew; *Nonna* Josephina, who was all proud and fancy; my mother, wearing her finest clothes; Celeste, my older sister, who came all the way from Milan; and I, who thought about Bellina and how sorry I was she couldn't be there with us.

Carlota was the first to shed a tear when Bruno read his section of the Torah, even though she did not understand the words. Apart from Maurizio, our knowledge of Hebrew was quite limited. But even without understanding the words of the prayers and blessings, each of us in that synagogue felt the shared Jewish comradeship. The war had lit the synagogue in a different light and enhanced the fact we were Jewish, but more than anything, the existence of Jerusalem. Suddenly, Jerusalem was a name of a real place and not just a word to call an abstract object that you yearn for.

When the UN resolution for the establishment of a Jewish state in the land of Israel was accepted in late November of 1947, Maurizio already had a date for visiting Tel Aviv and Jerusalem, as well as a planning a meeting with David Ben Gurion. Three illegal emigration ships that he helped purchase had arrived at the coast of Israel, where they were apprehended by the British authorities and sent to Cyprus. In every family gathering, Maurizio talked about emigrating to Israel, and each time he did, Michelangelo looked at me to see my reaction. One evening I dared to say I didn't want to go to Palestine and that I wished to live our lives in Biella.

"It won't help you," Maurizio said to me quietly. I tried to claim that Bruno could not be without us anymore.

He had enough with all that he went through, and he

answered that Bruno was fine. "He is grown up now, and the war is over. Until he graduates from school, he will live with his grandmother and uncles."

His plan was that we, together with the two younger children, would emigrate to Israel, and when Bruno graduated from school in Biella, he would join us. I felt in his tone of voice that he despised me for wanting to stay in the Europe that had betrayed us.

The period after the war is coming back to me now, when the disease is deforming me from the inside. It was the time I had nightmares. I felt most uncomfortable with my life. There was a couple we really adopted; Maurizio was the one who married them at the synagogue, after which he brought them to our home. The young refugee woman, who was very beautiful, told me a little of what she went through, how she escaped the camp when the war was over, and how she was chased by soldiers, how she finally managed to arrive at a convent and hid there. After that, she escaped to Berlin, where she met Haiden, who lost his entire family, and she came with him to Biella. They did not leave each other's side, always holding hands, and each time they started to speak, she cried as he was continuously holding her. They sat with me in my kitchen as I prepared meals for them while I listened to them say how they would go to Israel, wiping my tears and thanking God for having all my children and Maurizio with me.

I also remember looking at her, unable to understand where she found the strength—after losing her entire family after soldiers tried to rape her, after she starved and ran through the woods—to go on living.

In the dreams I had then, after the war, Bruno was hungry, persecuted, trying to speak but no words would come out, and in life—maybe Maurizio was right—Bruno looked all right. For the first time in his life, he found himself going to a normal school with boys and girls. He had friends, understood the schoolwork and even played nicely with his brothers and cousins. I would wake up in the morning—after having nightmares about starving Bruno, escaping his persecutors—to see him sitting at the table eating his breakfast before going to school, and every once in a while, even smiling.

Visita Dall'America
(Visitors from America)

A few months prior to Maurizio's trip to Israel, Emanuelle and Lina came with the kids to Italy for a visit. When we met, we fell into each other's arms. Celeste also came from Milan, and for a moment, it was like it used to be, three sisters going to visit their mother in Vercelli. The last time I visited Vercelli was before the war. This time, I had my three children with me—Bruno, Ricardo, and Aldo—and my two sisters had their children with them. I bought meat and vegetables at the market in Biella for Mother to cook for us, and the three of us boarded the train for Vercelli, carrying baskets and suitcases for the children.

Anetta, a little shorter than I remembered, waited for us at the train station, and held us longer than ever before, out of all the hugs she ever gave us. We stood there, three sisters with eight children at the Vercelli train station with all the rubble and indifferent people who usually fill train stations around us, and hugged Mother over and over again, as Lina and I kept tearing up. After the excitement had subsided a little, we started to walk toward the house. I showed my children the piazza where we used to spend our evenings, the shops where we bought our sewing tools, and where Alfredo liked to have his coffee. The streets I used to walk in as a child looked different to me. The shop windows I remembered being colorful and filled with desirable goods, were now old and faded.

Most of the stained windows in the synagogue we passed were destroyed, and a plaque had been added with the names of all the Jews that perished in the war, including Aunt Celeste, who wasn't killed by the Germans but died when passing through the mountains to Switzerland when she escaped to together with Anneta, assisted by Michelangelo. There, in the mountains, her heart failed her, and she passed away. Anneta remained in Switzerland with distant relatives, and when the war ended, she returned alone to an empty house.

Vercelli welcomed us, tired and neglected, as if time there stood still. My parents' house that Alfredo, my father, and Celeste, my aunt, never returned to looked darkened and distant.

We opened the house and the shutters, took out the dishes, and the kitchen was bustling. We had to hurry up and feed eight hungry children, and my mother, back to her old self, started ordering the three of us around, like in the old days.

Her hunched over stature looked a bit taller following out visit. With carefully picked words, she told us of her events, all the while in awe at her grandchildren. Aldo looks a little like Ricardo, and Bruno looks a little like Celeste's son. Anna reminded her a little of herself. Teary-eyed, Lina clung to her the whole time.

It was a true homecoming. We were able to talk about the death of our father, Alfredo, about the war, tell about the hunger, the refugee camp, and Aunt Celeste's demise in Switzerland. My mother was thrilled to host her grandchildren and us and, but it was clear that she had aged a great deal.

It was obvious to me she would not join us on our emigration to Palestine, and I did not want to upset her and ruin the excitement, so we hardly spoke of it. Celeste and her kids went ahead and returned to their home in Milan. Both Lina and I stayed for a few more days of sanity before returning home to Biella.

Emanuelle stood tall in America, and the more horrors of war stories he heard, the prouder he was for making the right decision. Lina, as beautiful and smiley as ever, was also a little fuller. She had an array of floral dresses and high-heeled shoes and seemed like she was floating on air from joy for being back in Italy. Her children tried to adjust. Anna, who was a baby when they left, did not remember her Italian. Sami and Alfred were in Italy, the country they heard so much about, for the first time. Their encounter with their cousins was natural and instant. It is incomprehensible, but Lina's and my children were much closer than to Celeste's kids. Aldo and Ricardo played with Sami and Alfred. Bruno was with Anna, blushing from time to time. There were moments I wished that time would stand still.

Above it all, Maurizio's trip to Israel was coming up, together with the meeting that was arranged for him with Ben Gurion. Around the table, they talked less about money and more about Israel.

Emanuelle and Maurizio bonded, the realization of the

worst Emanuelle anticipated and Maurizio's awakening and decision to leave Europe connected them. Emanuelle listened to Maurizio and his ideas for hours, as Alberto and Michelangelo kept busy with Michelangelo's new hobby—flying an airplane they had built themselves with parts ordered by Michelangelo from America. It seemed the level of stress brought on by the war was a level Michelangelo got used to being in. That was how the airplane came into our lives. They both started flying it in the Italian skies and dedicated their days and nights to it. There was a joke going around in our family that after we all emigrated to Israel, Michelangelo would come in his plane.

When we said good-bye to Lina and Emanuelle, who returned to America, it was agreed that when Maurizio came back from his trip to Israel, they, too, would join us in emigrating, and our families would relocate to live in Israel. Knowing that we were about to meet again and live our lives together made me very happy. In my conversations with God, I prayed it would be like this—that we would manage to meet again and raise our children together in a country where, as it was said, the sun was constantly shining and the oranges were orange, and not red like in Italy. I had something to hope for.

I packed Maurizio's suitcase singing songs. New shirts were starched, gray suits were fitted to his size, and the meetings with Ben Gurion, Yehuda Arazi and the rest of the important people we read about in the paper, excited me as well. The plan was for him to arrive in Tel Aviv, meet with Ben Gurion, contemplate the businesses that would be suited for him to open in Israel, and decide the area where we would purchase our apartment. After that it was planned, he would travel to Jerusalem to see the city and visit distant relatives that waited for him, the Otolangi family.

On the morning of his departure, the children lined up to bid their father farewell. They were all speaking Hebrew by then, and I received a strong hug and very energetic look from Maurizio. "See you in three weeks," he said and the previous night's memory tickled me inside. Lina's visit and his trip had taken us back to our loving days, and I had many hours in which I didn't feel guilty about Bruno, and I could be content with what I had.

Michelangelo came to take Maurizio to the train station, and Alberto tagged along. They were very close and discussed Michelangelo's new girlfriend, a tall blonde who resided in Rome, and said that they should fly out to visit her and bring her to Biella. We waved good-bye. I followed them with my eyes—three elegant men driving away, disappearing from sight.

C'e Stato Un Incidente
(An Accident Happened)

I will never forget the 26th of October, 1948.

While Maurizio was on his first visit to Israel, his two brothers, Alberto and Michelangelo would come and visit, and eat our meals with us. Alberto came with his daughters and Michelangelo with the fragrance of a single man. Since Maurizio had gone, even Michelangelo started talking about emigrating to Israel, and the thought that he would come and live there with us made me very happy.

On Friday, the 24th of October, right when Michelangelo came to us for dinner, Maurizio sent a telex message that he was in Tel Aviv and there was only one normal road there, and that people traveled mainly by carts, but that the air was clear and the sea was very beautiful. He wrote that when he returned, he would tell us more. Everyone was so thrilled that I had no more room to object anymore. Italy had become a place you say good-bye to.

At the end of the meal, Michelangelo finished his coffee and placed the cup in the sink, lifted six-year-old Aldo and walked around the house with him on his shoulders. Ricardo threw a ball to Aldo, and he caught it and threw it back to him. Both kids played throwing the ball to one another, and Michelangelo narrated the game as if he were a sports broadcaster on the radio, "Ricardo pitches the ball that was now blocked, and he is attempting another attack…" The children were laughing so hard, Carlota wiped her hands on her apron and laughed, too, and Bruno added names of famous players to the descriptions.

When it became late, Michelangelo bid us farewell, and we made plans to meet for lunch the next day. I knew Alberto and he were planning to fly to Rome in the morning and asked him to bring wine for lunch.

With all of my inner emotions and my pacts with God, I was preoccupied with Maurizio and his visit to Israel only. There were talks about Arab gangs that ambushed and attacked Jews, and there were rumors about car accidents because the roads were so faulty. That was why I promised God that if Maurizio came home safely, and indeed Lina came to live with me in Israel, I would double the number of good deeds and light *Shabbat* candles every Friday. Every night, while mumbling the *Shma Israel* prayer, I negotiated at length with God about the fact that Bruno was smiling, and what I was willing to do to keep the love flowing. It was the same that Friday night when I went to bed. Nothing could prepare me for what happened the next day.

We waited for them to come to lunch for over an hour and a half, and they never showed up. The Saturday slugged along. We ate with the kids and left a plate for my two brothers-in-law if they showed up. I told the children to play quietly as Carlota, and I retired to our bedrooms for a rest.

The sound of footsteps coming to the front door made me jump from my bed. It was Alberto, who came in without knocking on the door, passed through the living room, limping and with a black and blue shiner covering his right eye, and went straight into the kitchen. Without saying a word, he sat in the kitchen and signaled me to send the children away. I looked straight at him trying to understand what happened. His face was gray, and his leg was bandaged.

The airplane... The thought grabbed my stomach.

"It was cloudy on the way to Rome," he said. "We couldn't see well. The plane crashed into a mountain. Michelangelo was killed instantly."

In the telegram we sent to Maurizio, there were two words, "Call please." You do not deliver news of death in a telegram, we all agreed. The first death my children knew was of their beloved uncle. After that accident, Lina and Emanuelle stopped traveling together. Even to the funeral, they flew separately, and I swore to myself that none of my children would ever fly in an airplane that they themselves were piloting.

I don't remember much from the funeral, only that I cried a lot. Michelangelo was a big part of our lives. He was like a big brother to the children, and to me, he was more than a brother-in-law. I felt guilty. I really did dream about him a lot.

Maurizio came back shocked. Everything looked so perfect and successful. The trip to Israel was a thrilling experience for him, and then tragedy struck and severed it.

During the entire seven days of mourning—*Shiva*—the discussion revolved around Israel. The next trip over there was already planned, and it was agreed that this time, I would join Maurizio and we would buy an apartment there. Still, instinctively, each time they talked about Israel, I searched for Michelangelo's expression.

Nonna Josephina, wearing Michelangelo's watch, hovered around Bruno as usual. He was due to stay in Italy to finish his studies at the Academic School of Textile. It was discussed that Emanuelle and Lina would return to America immediately after the *Shiva*, and once Maurizio the two children and I got settled in Israel, they would come, too. Maurizio described a very practical meeting he had with David Ben Gurion that took place "not far from Tel Aviv," (at a place that is nowadays Ramat Aviv).

In that meeting, Maurizio was offered to recruit more affiliates for the purpose of building a hotel there that would be called "Hotel Ramat Aviv." Those who arranged the meeting and took part in it were his new friends from his activities for the benefit of the Jewish Refugees—Yehuda Arazi and Ada Sereni, the widow of Haim Enzo Sereni.[6] The Vitale family

---

6   In the beginning of 1944, Enzo Sereni volunteered to parachute behind the German lines in Italy to establish contact with the Jews who survived there. On 15 May 1944, after he parachuted, all communication with him was lost. When World War II ended, and Enzo wasn't among the prisoners who returned, Ada Sereni approached Shaul Meirov (eventually Avigur), the head of the Immigration Institute, and with his approval, went to Italy to try and trace the fate of her husband. At that time, her three children remained in Givat Brener. The search for her husband ended when she found written evidence, according to which Enzo Sereni was

was most excited by the fact that Ben Gurion offered the land near Tel Aviv to build a hotel the likes of which had never been seen before in Israel.

It was clear to Maurizio that his brothers would be partners with him. After the lineup of the hotel was consolidated as a compound of small houses with a pool and a banquette hall in the middle, and the cost of construction was established, he turned to raise the capital needed from the Jewish capitalists such as Mayer, Rothchild from South Africa, and others he managed to infect with his enthusiasm. Maurizio succeeded in gathering quite a large group of capitalists that gave him their trust, and they all signed on and contributed to this enterprise.

In the year 1952, four years after the idea for establishing the hotel came to be, the hotel was built. Maurizio, our two young boys, and I emigrated two years before then, in 1950.

---

executed at the Dachau Concentration Camp in November of 1944. At the same time, she met Yehuda Arazi, who coordinated the emigration institution's activities in Italy, and accepted the offer to join the mission. From June 1945 until the establishment of the state of Israel, **Sereni** acted in Italy, first as Arazi's vice president and then (from April 1947) as the Chief of the Mossad in Italy. During that period, the Mossad managed to launch over 20,000 immigrants on dozens of ships that made their way from various sites along the Italian coast.

Immigrati
(Willing Immigrants)

"It will be good for Mother, too, if Bruno stays with her lon-ger," Maurizio said to me. Everyone was very worried about *Nonna* Josephina, who had lost her son. Josephina bravely embraced Bruno and said it gave her a reason to get up in the morning.

Getting ready to emigrate, with all that it entailed—buying plane tickets and organizing everything—made Bruno's re-maining in Italy for the time being almost obvious.

I decided that if we were really leaving Italy, I would show Aldo and Ricardo Rome before we left. I took Bruno with me as well, and together, we had a farewell from Rome trip. Rome was luminous, but the horrors of war were visible and showed there, too. Here and there, were ruined homes, and the Jewish area looked shell-shocked. The Jews in Rome walked quickly, looking straight ahead. I could see vacant looks on some of them. This is the look of someone who knows he's hanging between life and death; I knew that look from myself. It's a hollow gaze as if you are in one place looking at an inner movie from another.

As far as I was concerned, Michelangelo's death was the

end of our era in Italy. The thought of how everything was sensitive and changing did not leave me. He—the only one that made me feel comfortable about my doubts regarding Israel—did not see the mountain and crashed to his death. His crash also pulverized my doubt and made me give in to Maurizio. I was angry at Italy, in which my father died, and my mother aged alone. The country that allowed the Germans to loot our property enabled them to outlaw its Jews—to deport, murder, and annihilate them. The Holocaust made us understand we would never feel safe in Italy again. And so, we packed ourselves and emigrated to Israel with Aldo, Ricardo, and Carlota.

On the first day of our arrival, we went to the beach with its white sands. To our joy, it was really close to the Dan Hotel where we stayed until the furniture we shipped from Italy arrived at our apartment at 38 Dizengoff Street.

Our first home in Israel was at 38 Dizengoff Street, and that is where Ricardo and Aldo met their first friends, the Diamant family, who immigrated from Belgium and remained our very close friends to this day.

The first year in Israel was like a dream with lots of dust and very little butter. I waited for Lina the entire time. A few months after we had settled, Lina, Emanuelle, and the children arrived and attempted to live in Israel, but the years of austerity that welcomed them caused them to return to their lives in America. So did Alberto, who had returned to Italy and continued to run the family's textile factory. Nora and Paula, Alberto's daughters, lived in Israel with their children and felt very much at home at my place. Paula married Julio, who had his *Bar Mitzvah* after the war together with Bruno.

All along, every summer, the sisters—Lina, Celeste, and I—would meet at the Hotel Royal in Courmayeur, an enchanting ski resort at the foot of the Mont Blanc in Italy. This reunion became especially important to us after my mother passed away at her home in our hometown in 1951. We arrived at our reunion from three different continents, Tel Aviv, Milan and New York. There were times when the children and grandchildren joined us.

Each time we had to say good-bye, we would sob like I did when Lina left for America. Indeed, the farewells, despite the telephones and all the means of communication available, were difficult for us.

Tel Aviv
(Building a Home in Tel Aviv)

Israel, in its years of establishment, welcomed us with austerity and harsh living conditions. All who we wished would live next to us could not last in the country. Even Carlota went back to Italy. But in fact, because of the difficult life we had, new social connections were formed. We all stood in line with coupons in a kind of immigrants' comradeship. In this way, it turned out we had many friends from Salonika and from many other places.

From the moment we settled in our apartment at 38 Dizengoff Street, Bruno made regular visits to Israel, and when he graduated in 1953, he emigrated there. By then, he had connections with several families that arrived from Italy as well, and we had found a beautiful woman from the Serbadio family for Bruno. The wedding was held at the Ramat Aviv Hotel together with the family and the community of friends we had around us. I found myself thanking the Lord we all managed to stay healthy and intact.

I was a full partner in the hotel from its establishment. I was the hotel's bookkeeper and sat behind the accounting desk in the room next to reception for many years.

The sixties and seventies of the twentieth century were very good for the Ramat Aviv Hotel. It was central in its location and in its experience. Many celebrities came to stay in it, and many came to its swimming pool. A great number of people chose to celebrate social and family events there, and of course, our family's many events and weddings took place there, too.

These days, a street named after Maurizio Vitale exists in the neighborhood established next to the hotel, thanks to our son, Reuven (Ricardo), who acted to properly commemorate his father's life's work. It's too bad the sign doesn't say what a multi-talented entrepreneur Maurizio was. He did not confine himself only to the hotel he built or to running the family textile factory that remained in Italy and was orchestrated by Alberto, to which he traveled twice a year. In 1958, Maurizio decided he needed to manufacture wool for knitting and for the textile industry in Israel and entered into a partnership with the Strugo family. The name the partners gave to their new enterprise was "Vitalgo," which was a combination of their two family names—Vitale and Strugo.

As usual, when Maurizio decided to do something, the wheels started turning. Bruno purchased the lot with a phone call to Maurizio in Italy, and immediately the machines were bought, and an architect was brought in to plan the structure; within two years, the Vitalgo plant was built.

Maurizio and the three boys worked in the factory throughout the years of its existence and were pioneers of the Israeli industry. Many families worked in the plant, and from its first day, the peace Maurizio believed in existed in it. Arabs and Jews worked together side by side next to the machines and were part of the creation.

A few years after we emigrated to Israel, Maurizio suffered his first heart attack, after which the doctors strongly recommended he stop smoking and engage in sports. He returned to work fairly quickly, left the office and started strolling among the machines. He abandoned the cigarettes and continued to live a healthy productive life in Israel up until the end. He passed away at the age of seventy-eight after falling ill with a kidney disease. Maurizio was too proud to accept becoming a burden and didn't want to live with a disability. The last time he was hospitalized, he hinted to me that he would not be coming home. The way he ran his life was the way he managed his death as well.

Everyone, the entire family and close friends that used to participate in our weddings and celebrations in the center of the Vitale family life we created in that country, came to his funeral and *Shiva* in Tel Aviv.

Throughout our life together, from the moment I first laid eyes on him, my love for Maurizio pushed aside everything else. I loved my children, but their father came first. In the months prior to Maurizio's death, I stopped sleeping altogether. My concern about him and the understanding he would probably die before me created such anxiety in me that it would not allow me to close my eyes. I loved him more than I loved myself. He was the center of my world. I adored him and dreaded my life without him. Throughout the *Shiva*, I could not fall asleep, and when I rose from mourning on the seventh day, I knew—my life from then on would never be the same. With Maurizio gone, my heart emptied, and a great deal of space was opened up for my children, their children, and many, many memories.

Grazie Alla Vita
(Thanks to Life)

And now, the end is near.

I have been sitting in Maurizio's armchair since morning, in front of which the grandchildren would line up to wish him *Shabbat Shalom* when they came to visit on a Friday, and I'd make them my pasta with tomato sauce. "You have the best tomato sauce in the world, Grandma," my granddaughter used to say. I cooked with fresh tomatoes and basil, just like my mother did, and I would add salt only at the end together with a little sugar.

It's been a few long weeks since I tasted pasta. My tumor doesn't like food. I am losing weight. I am thirsty but unable to drink, and no voice is coming out. My stomach hurts all the time. I need to take an orange pill, which stops the pain immediately—together with my thoughts.

I hear the elevator. It seems that Bruno is coming. It makes me happy. The telephone rings, but I can't talk anymore. I hear them answering it. My girlfriends want to visit: Mrs. Albo, Mrs. Serbadio, Mrs. Havkin. I am ashamed to let them see me like this, in this state.

My ribs are sticking out. I have never been so thin, not

even in the refugee camp in Switzerland when the guilt first started gnawing at me. My body is eating itself from the inside. The guilt that hid in the mounts of my body all these years has taken over and is winning. I hardly have any hair, and it's white and thin. My body is wrinkled and beaten, and inside the tumor is celebrating—celebrating all the thoughts I didn't want to think. Conquering all the nights I managed to fall asleep and not consider any decisions.

Now, I hear the garbage trucks at night backing up, I feel the tumor growing inside me, feel the end approaching.

I deserve this. What kind of mother leaves her child alone in the midst of war? What kind of mother leaves her sick son in the hospital's isolation ward for months? How could I allow Maurizio to decide to send him to boarding school and still keep making love with him when my child was in isolation at a hospital in Switzerland? Maurizio was the one who made all the decisions. I complied with them, and now my body is punishing me for it.

A couple of days after Maurizio's Shiva, they discovered the tumor really close to my heart. It was my daughter-in-law who came with me to the doctor, and he, without sparing any details, placed the word "cancer" on the table.

In the past five years, all the treatments and coping with the disease have taken me back to that war.

The disease connected me with the war, that because of or thanks to it, I am here, in Israel. I think—thanks to.

I was afraid of the country of Israel, just like I was afraid during the war. That far away land was a strange world to me, and I only wished to get my life before the war back. I wanted to go home, wished for my children's naïve childhood, wanted to bring back the innocence and smile to Bruno's eyes.

Everyone thinks that I am losing my mind because, suddenly, I am talking about the war. Only Bruno collaborates with me. Ricardo and Aldo were too young to remember. Bruno remembers, but his memories and mine are not the same. He admits to me that the end of the war was his salvation. Bruno smiles now. I am trying to figure out whether he is smiling to please me or he is really happy. He is a grown man now and still hasn't let go of the need to please me.

My eyes are closed, the pain shoots through my body, but Bruno manages to make me laugh. He reminds me of how Aldo and Ricardo squabbled on the carpet in my bright living room, like young puppies. They continued to quarrel when they grew up, too. There's a glazier out there who built himself a home from all the doors they smashed during their fights. They grew up together, and there's a certain intimacy between them that allows drama, for doors to get smashed, and for life to continue.

Bruno is cautious and pulls away when conflict arises. I am looking at him through the slits of my partially shut eyes; a man of almost fifty, dressed elegantly, who holds himself up with a pride reserved only for successful men. I wonder if he talked about the war with his wife and daughters. Is he sharing his pain?

The nurse's rubber soles are squeaking on the polished floors, the rhythm reminds me of the stepping sounds around the camp. Maurizio was bribing the Swiss guards to find Bruno for me. I carry the burden of guilt for Maurizio, his father, too. Maurizio, who later built him a factory and made sure he had a good life, but first abandoned him during the war.

The light is too bright; I can barely keep my body inside the armchair. The morning nurse, the one whose name I can't remember, turned on the television to see if it will rain today. The sound needs to be turned down. She is entering the room again, bringing with her the scent of the cigarette she just smoked in the kitchen. It reminds me of the first cigarette I smoked with Maurizio after the *Shabbat* dinner at his parents' house, about a month after we were married.

If only I could once again stand in my laundry corner and smoke, stand and talk to Lina in our native language, Italian. I miss her lively voice. The last time we spoke, she cried. I told her I was dying, and she is deliberating whether to come from New York to say good-bye. The doctor told Aldo, my youngest son, that there is still time, so he decided to leave for a week's holiday, skiing. It reassured Lina a little. If he went on his trip, it probably meant there is still time.

I have lived in Israel for forty years and still feel like an Italian. Possibly, you belong to the place you were born until the day you die. I know my death is imminent. I know the cancer inside me is eating me alive and that my life without Maurizio is not as good as it used to be with him.

I hear the elevator, and the phone is ringing, too. It is probably one of the grandchildren or daughters-in-law, who want to know what to bring. If I had stayed in bed, the entire crowd would have invaded our bedroom, where a remnant of Maurizio's scent still remained. It is good that I am in the armchair in the dining room. They—my family—are sitting around the table exchanging looks, and I can see their pity and despair.

I am fortunate they are here around me; my mother died alone. In the end, that is all that's left—family and friends.

I am sorry. I want to tell them that I am sorry. I did not want to die like this, thin and weak, without my hairdresser, without my hair, without my makeup. Like an old woman. All these years, I thought that when I reached the end of the road, I would have the courage to die with elegance. It seems I still have a little zest for life, even though all that remains of this life is excruciating stomach pains.

Where is the doctor? I need him to come with the orange pills; the pills that sooth my pain and thoughts.

My lucidity comes and goes. I recognize and don't recognize my visitors, and every once in a while, I can see sights of family and friends in my eyes, as if they are arising from my memory.

I worked as an accountant at the Ramat Aviv Hotel for many years. The accounting I did at my work was a reflection of the inner accountancy I did in my life, which was a part of it and caused by the war. I could never explain to anyone a mother's difficulty to leave a child. Each grandchild born brought tears to my eyes, as I remembered my difficulties as a new mother. I now feel, as I am on my deathbed, that I want to apologize to Bruno for my weakness, for giving in to Maurizio, and for leaving him by himself, a boy of eleven years old, during the war.

Many years later, even when he grew up, I always felt like

an inadequate mother to him.

When I look around, I can see that I am no longer at home. I can also vaguely remember being taken away and meeting Maurizio for a split second, and then I came back for a few more days. It is clear to me now that I am bidding farewell. Aldo will not be able to be here on time. I am hooked to many tubes and devices, and Bruno's daughters are with me in the room, as if signaling to me he will forgive me when he reads the final words I wish to say to him. I hope that my boys will be able to establish successful families like their father did. I hope their wives will be as I was to their father, who as far as I was concerned, always came first.

I regret now I didn't have a daughter—no daughter I could teach the secrets of love to, the ability to love oneself and from there the ability to love your partner. My love for Maurizio was greater than my love for myself. If I had the chance to start over, I would still live my life with Maurizio, but I would listen to myself more.

Since he passed away, I miss him so much. Finally, I am meeting him. Here we are, traveling by train, and he is sitting next to me saying, "You see, Tu? Life had changed. It is not possible to stay in Europe after this war. We will emigrate to Israel. This name, which is in the bible and is seemingly connected only to the past and future is becoming part of our present. We will live there. I wish that Alberto, Michelangelo, and Emanuelle would join us."

I only manage to utter one word: "Bruno…"

Maurizio leans back, crossing his long legs anew, thin and pale, he lights a cigarette. "I hope that Bruno is learning and promoting himself to be a responsible understanding adult. He is the eldest, and has a great responsibility to continue leading the family."

I am crying, "Bruno, what have you done to Bruno?"

Maurizio is looking at me, and I can see the freckles next to his eyes. "Don't cry, TO. I know you were angry with me about Bruno. I know how hard it was for you when we left Bruno without us with my mother for over a year. You were angry about that, too. True, I know my mother never took care of me or my brothers like you did of our children. I know my brothers thought I was insane. I know there were many people that, because of you, continued to speak with me. I know I was stubborn, and no one could convince me, but I saw you, and I heard you."

We are both sitting together on the train as if we never parted, and I am listening to Maurizio, who found the right time to tell me what he never said during our life together. He is beautiful to me, and my love for him is growing by the minute.

"The war changed my way of thinking and my way of life. Immigrating to Israel was the move I am most proud of, from all the moves I did during my life. Our sons, Reuven and Eldad, also speak Hebrew beautifully. They emigrated at such an age, when it was still easy for them to learn. Bruno, too, spoke Hebrew later, and I am very pleased by the fact all my grandchildren speak Hebrew.

"They, at the Histadrut Labor Foundation, called me a capitalist. It is correct. I didn't like the communists who wished to divide everything equally. I couldn't grasp the idea of the *kibbutz.* I couldn't understand how everyone lived together like that. True, it is a fact that without the *kibbutz* settlements, the State of Israel could not have been established, but I believe in a free market. I believe we each need to work and enjoy the fruits of our labor. I tried to teach my kids the same values. I tried to pass on to my sons the value of the connection between siblings—the connection which bonds the bond which allows you to say what's in your heart, the kind in which one look is enough to explain everything. I wasn't afraid to be perceived as a lunatic. I was the crazy brother, and my brothers thought differently than me. After we were left without Michelangelo, the three of us acted in benefit of the three of us, and we were partners in everything we did.

"When my boys grew up, I wondered to myself if my father loved us equally. I made every effort to love equally and did everything to make the relationships between my children good, that they would understand the power brotherhood holds. We had many arguments. My children said much more to me than I ever dared to say to my father, and I am positive their children will say even more. You, TO always listened to our children, but in the end accepted my decisions without fail and followed them through. That was what gave me the strength to do all that I did. I am grateful to you. You made me happy with your love."

Before I managed to reply, Maurizio was gone. Our journey ended. I hope that my grandchildren and great-grandchildren will learn from our story, that the most important thing in life—is love.

On the 1st of December, 2009, the relatives of Carlota

Rizetto received the honorary certificate that honored her and her deeds during the Holocaust, with the Righteous Gentiles. For putting her life at risk to save persecuted Jews from those who sought to harm them. Her name is forever perpetuated on the honorary board at the Righteous among Nations Grove in Yad Vashem.

Epilogue

My grandmother was born more than 100 years ago, in 1912. I was her fifth grandchild. Before me, four granddaughters were born, and after me came the twins, Nir and Limor, my cousins. After they were born, our family only had boys. When my grandmother passed away in 1990, she already had ten grandchildren and two great-grandchildren. Today, the two great-granddaughters, Daniella and Maya, have cute children of their own, Itay and Gali.

In the twenty-six years that have passed since my grandmother, Vittoria, died, I have found myself talking to her quite a lot in my heart. In the years that have gone by, I, too, had three boys and almost no one from our grandparents' generation remains; certainly each of them deserves to be remembered, but I chose Vittoria, or maybe she chose me.

From the day I was born, I felt I was born well. I grew up in a family that made family its first priority. It is nice to grow up in a family that feels, and is, successful, a family that loves traveling to Italy, likes good food, and in general, believes in living the good life. In our family, aside from boycotting products that originated in Germany, the Holocaust wasn't discussed.

My grandmother, Vittoria, raised three children and a

husband with polished shoes, and maintained relationships with two sisters and dozens of cousins and friends.

When I began investigating her story, I discovered that a great number of people loved her and told me tales of her generosity, of her ability to bring people together, and especially of her extraordinary love for Maurizio.

Up until a year before she passed away, my grandmother worked as an accountant at the Ramat Aviv Hotel. She drove everywhere in an Italian car with great confidence and ran her many assistants fearlessly.

As a child, I felt just like all the other grandchildren, equal among equals. In the years I went to the high school next to my grandmother's house in Tel Aviv, I used to go there for lunch with her and my grandfather, for whom, until the day he died, *Nonna* would make exactly, and with great attention, the food he loved. They used to eat together. Those meals were important. During those years, I became very close to her. I loved the smell of her cigarettes. I loved the mints that came after the cigarettes, the chocolates, the scent of the silver dish polish, and the smell of the wooden furniture polish.

This book seeks to tell her story, to illuminate her character. It is a story of a hundred years that began in a small town in Italy and goes through the war in Europe, until it arrives in Israel, creating a new reality.

It is a story about the epic love that existed between her and Maurizio, my grandfather. A love that I, as a mother of three and a wife, am trying to understand how to hold on to for so many years, and which holds no doubt.

The year 1990, in which my grandmother passed away,

was also the year I had my end-of-service trip overseas. In preparation for my trip, the forms for textile studies at the Leeds University were almost automatically filled out. My father graduated there as a textile engineer, and it was only natural I would follow his lead and continue the path her father laid out. There's a textile factory, a firm, and we need to man the trenches. Even as kids, all of the cousins spent their summer holidays working at the plant, packing wool, answering the phones, being in the shadow of the founding and expanding generation. We had family pride, and the arts and crafts teachers in all of our schools got to receive leftover wool and teach how to make pompons.

So, ten days after my grandmother passed away due to a cruel disease, I found myself at the gates of the Leeds University campus. I had to finalize registration, and immediately after my trip, uproot my life to Leeds.

The distance, the cold, the English, and textile did not appeal to me. Already on the train from London, next to my friend Galia, I felt I wasn't sure I wanted to be there in the rain and cold, and the welcoming chimneys of Leeds with the black smoke coming out of them contributed to my doubts.

After two nights of soul searching, I stood in a payphone booth and called my father at the factory. His favorite telephone operator put the call through as I told him excitedly that I was canceling the plan, and that he could register me for anything I would be accepted in at the University of Tel Aviv. I wanted to continue traveling, knowing I would return to a place where the sun was shining, and I had a hunch that despite the disappointment I was causing then, it was better for me. The call went through O.K. and I kept on with my trip having the concern he would not be welcoming me with open arms. In hindsight, I was at peace with the decision.

The dining room table at my house is round. It is the same dining room table that was at my grandmother's house in Italy, and then in Israel. Around a round table, so I've learned during the years I've studied the world of management, there is no hierarchy and no pre-set seats. Only *Nono Maurizio* had a fixed place at this table, next to the chocolate drawer.

I tried to tell the story of this woman, and of the family that grew around her. I met with my cousins and their cousins and sat for many hours with my one and only father, who helped, encouraged and supported me.

I allowed myself to follow her—and in truth, to catch up, imagine the unknown and incorporate them with known facts. Many great and exciting stories were edited out, and many important facts had vanished.

It all started in a writing workshop taught by Eshkol Nevo and Orit Gidly, through whom I met Michal, who tirelessly accompanied me on my way to the final version. On this occasion, I would like to thank Bruno, Ruthy, Ronnie, Nora, Paula, Julio, Reuven, my mother, Rachel, my father, Eldad (Aldo), and all who were a part of the research and the story, and Adi Hadas, Shirly, and Ruthy, who read the manuscript over and over again and never gave up.

I would like to extend my deepest thanks to the Israeli publishers from "Good Book", Ilan Levi and Elia Alon Hacohen, for the opportunity to meet and enjoy the editing abilities and wisdom of Edna Shabtai, who I thrilled to learn identified with Vittoria in an inspiring manner, understood the love, respected the romance and made my manuscript into the book it became for all to read.

With love and joy, I thank Mosh, who contained the entire process of investigation and writing, and is my partner for our three extraordinary sons, who to me are the true creation of life.

Dafna.